About the author

Crystal Joyce Townsend, is at the time of this publication 65, and proud of it! She was born in New York City when the moon was in Cancer. She is a poet and a Scottish Fold breeder. She lives with her husband, David, too many cats, a few Bonsai plants, and many flowers in a busy South Florida city on the New River… (although they constantly talk about moving to the mountains in a peaceful quiet hideaway town).

TORTITUDE

Crystal Joyce Townsend and
Gemini Townsend
───────────────────────────────

TORTITUDE

Vanguard Press

VANGUARD PAPERBACK

© Copyright 2024
Crystal Joyce Townsend and Gemini Townsend

The right of Crystal Joyce Townsend and Gemini Townsend to be identified as author of
this work has been asserted by them in accordance with the Copyright, Designs and Patents Act 1988.

All Rights Reserved

No reproduction, copy or transmission of this publication
may be made without written permission.
No paragraph of this publication may be reproduced,
copied or transmitted save with the written permission of the publisher, or in accordance with the provisions
of the Copyright Act 1956 (as amended).

Any person who commits any unauthorised act in relation to this publication may be liable to criminal prosecution and civil claims for damages.

A CIP catalogue record for this title is available from the British Library.

ISBN 978-1-80016-868-8

This is a work of fiction. Names, characters, businesses, places, events and incidents are either the products of the author's imagination or used in a fictitious manner. Any resemblance to actual persons, living or dead, or actual events is purely coincidental.

Vanguard Press is an imprint of
Pegasus Elliot Mackenzie Publishers Ltd.
www.pegasuspublishers.com
First Published in 2024

Vanguard Press
Sheraton House Castle Park
Cambridge England

Printed & Bound in Great Britain

Dedication

This book is dedicated to Caprice Townsend, the founder of Montessori Cats and to my sister, Lynne Decker who encouraged me to share the tale

Acknowledgements

I would like to thank the Montessori Cats Cattery Cats who were inspired to share their secrets with their people and especially to Gemini, the leader of our Cats

Part 1
Getting Centered

The New Introduction

This guide was begun a few years ago, when life was oh so busy, with the way life can be for people... and the guides were put on the side capturing magical dust in the shadows... That is the way magic is often misplaced in life by people. It happens all too often, and is lost forever.

I was constantly reminded to return to it, by a very insistent and courageous lady... my sister Lynne, whose wise counsel I did not frequently take. Then came the Coronavirus, that has changed the way people see the world. The world needs healing forces, and new ways of being more than ever. Guides, like this one. Cat adoption at Montessori Cats Scottish Fold Cattery starting leaping high as people sensed that a cat by their side really helped them get through the days of social isolation and grief.

This was always so. Cats have been pawing out wisdom, and love and purrs... since the old days of Ancient Egypt, where they were understood to be divine presences. Today the cats are all busier than ever in these challenging days. They will continue to help by our side as we rebuild our world together.

Then my sister Lynne died. She was an artist and a bit of a butterfly. Somehow I did not expect her death to really happen, although she was fighting end stage cancer. Her soul is now opening in another realm. I miss her lots, but I hear her calling me to finish the guides.

So I am dedicating the completion of this project to Lynne, dancing with her white cat Charmian, until we meet again… I will use the wisdom in these guides now for myself, too.

The Old Introduction

This book is both a guide, and a celebration of living... life, with greater sensitivity to the pauses between the paws. Through the guides you will be led to a renaissance of your soul, found in ancient semi-lost secrets, passed down by queen cats to their kittens. These secrets are captured forever in an invisible realm, in the silent creaky spaces hidden behind the thoughts and activities of ordinary life. It is a little like entering an enchanted dream. Welcome inside...

We will help you create a soft and subtle shift in awareness taught by one who understands how very much people need more guidance in living a life charmed with richer, more velvety qualities. This is a tortoiseshell cat's purr and whisper manual. You have come upon it by chance, you think... Think again! There is serendipity at work here. You have come upon it by the good fortune of a magical encounter. To find a copy you must have been touched by the magical path of a tortoiseshell cat and her rays of Tortitude sometime in your last nine lives. Ah... Tortitude... Let me explain how this little book can expand... your quality of life and deeply transform you, without asking you to spend a single penny. Such a gift, of essential wonders… is hard to come upon in our modern world. You are most fortunate in this simple but dazzling discovery.

Sit back, and enjoy the ride… into a journey of bold elegance and hidden wisdoms I call Tortitude. It is an enchantment that can gently blossom the core of your life into a new realm of radiance and a subtle but profound awareness, confidence and satisfaction.

Before I begin, let me take this time to give credit to the inspirations of this guide. Gemini is the tortoiseshell cat, who decided to share the secrets of her kind. Caprice, the mother of Montessori Cats Cattery created the environment where we think the best cats in the word come from. Although Caprice is now in spirit, she still lovingly haunts our beloved cattery. She also inspires our dreams.

Tortitude is looking at life with eight pointed stars in your fully open eyes, and knowing when to half close them with an inner serenity. We will ponder many thoughts with you, and teach you pathways from paw ways in a human and therefore simpler form. Please be patient. Patience is ever so important, and a close cousin to good listening skills in all the ways of hunting.

Many folks will tell you to breathe deeply to be more fully present in the moment. This is fine advice, to be sure… However, we would like you to take it one paw step further out. Deeper breathing is often easy to talk about, but hard to actually experience for any length of time. You are about to enter the land of the alchemist cat. This guide will teach you how to attain an inner elegance, a mysterious presence that will carry you beyond the ordinary life via a bit of a magic carpet ride, into the extraordinary.

All of this without cost. All you need is the guide, and a little time spent with a special tortoiseshell cat named Gemini. Gemini says to tell you it is not really necessary to have a tortoiseshell cat of your own. She feels the guide alone is enough. This is the only time that I, Crystal, the channel writer, will strongly object. In my opinion, do get a cat to read the guide with. Like perfume it will create an ambiance that will prove to be an invaluable asset. Yes, any cat will help, but none as much as a tortoise shell Scottish fold. The folded ears are really rather cute, but optional. Straight ear Scottish fold cats have the same special spirits

This book is divided into guides to organize key points and turnabouts. It can be read in any direction, which is true of all magical writings. The chapters are not ordered by their importance in any direction. Their numbers are for organizational purposes alone, although there are some numerological thoughts I will point out along the journey. There are two exceptions, that being the first and the last. We suggest reading the first chapter to begin your journey, to engage the proper spirit. The last melts the alchemy together, into the finest of transformational ethers. So read the last chapter at the end.

You will read many fine books in your life. You will never forget this enchanted one. It can be read in a day, but the magic begins when you finish the guides, and its messages weaves into your inner life. That cannot be measured in time as it is a timeless, dateless journey of pure soul. Just read and surrender to the energetic shifts that will sweep you away. Sometimes it happens in your sleep, like a dream. Other times weeks will pass, and the magic will suddenly pull you outside and beyond your ordinary self.

A journey through infinity awaits you. We hope you enjoy the secrets shared with you now from the times when cats were worshipped as goddesses. This book is best read on a windy night, but it can be read any time and place that is quiet, and a bit out of the way of the ordinary. There was one reported case of a very sensitive person who never even read the book. She simply slept with it under her pillow, and her life was never the same…

The First Guide, The Guide to Elegance and Fine Feathers

As anyone can tell you, who truly understands elegance… it is an inner presence that expands outward in waves. These waves mesmerize like an enchanted charm. I must warn you, do not try to understand the meaning of these whispers on a logical, more intellectual level. That would never do. Just allow them to embrace and shower you softly with their secrets like a mist. Most everyone can sense the shimmer of elegance, however challenging it may be to define in words. If you try to hold onto it, it will evaporate like a mysterious vapor into the intangible. It is beyond wearing a certain fashion, which can change with the season like a flute on the wind… Fashion is interesting. It is a colorful discussion we will tackle later on in the guide. But it is definitely not elegance. Elegance is not about aligning with the times. It is about being, unique, to yourself. In order to express your inner elegance as we cats like to call it, you have to be alive and feel really special… deeply within yourself. We cats will show you how to reach within. Do not have any concerns with that whatsoever… if you are a bit lost. Truth be told, we rather expect you are.

Cats are timeless creatures, with our own unique set of rules and destiny. At Montessori Cattery for Scottish Folds, Crystal often says the right kitten goes to the right person at the right time. Kind of like, kitten kismet. We agree... For now just relax and trust the guides. You do not have to do anything for this journey. You do not need any special degrees or bank accounts or passwords to enter. We are taking you to a distant sacred land, beyond the ordinary paths you frequent. Just smile, and know you have brought a rare magic into your life. Anything is now possible, if you allow this guide to lead you... through some of the most uncharted spaces and timeless realms.

Do get ready to leap...

Cashmere mentioned you might want to get a manicure, or scratch something silky to get in the mood, before we begin...

(Cashmere is a long hair cream stud boy, who made some of the sweetest kittens in Florida.) That is up to you. This is not his book, but I thought I would mention his suggestion. It may help someone out there... If you feel inspired, do it.

All cats know secrets. We can teach much of it to you if you learn how to listen to us. There are some limits, as you are not a true cat, at least not in this life... Happily there are not many limits at all, except for the ones you create in your mind. We can help you through those rather easily if you so wish, and actually plan to do so in a latter chapter. If you can't wait, check out Shelly's spider web unknit mediation now. It is at the back of the book, so you can easily find it.

To begin, sit in the sunshine... and really tune in and listen to yourself. Go to a quiet place, without phones or news, music or talking... and be all alone with the silence. The one exception is you can bring your cat. This can be an indoor or outside space. You can sit by a moving stream, or just imagine one. You can go outside, and imagine yourself in a medieval castle or within an oak tree fairy land. There are no limits or references. You will know the right place by intuition. We will help you develop it. Just sit and listen to yourself... beyond the everyday chatter. You have to listen to your breath, body, mind and soul, and then listen deeper still with no expectations. You are not on a timer. You can practice every day or once a week... for a few minutes or hours. It can vary week to week. Learn to flow, with flexibility and allow yourself to change your routine and hunting grounds.

You may not be totally comfortable with some of the things you notice along the way, such as iguanas or old memories. We do guarantee if you keep going you will reach beyond them. You will start to melt, and transcend ordinary consciousness. It's a little like climbing a mountain before sunrise. It can be rough, dark and sometimes cold... but... on the top, when you finally arrive, embracing perseverance... all that remains, is beauty and light, and a glowing brilliance of color. That is who you really are deep inside. Wow!

That is the soul of your true essence… you can find yourself, in a shimmering sparkle, a brilliant glowing light, a globe of color and shine… more beautiful than a rare diamond. When you arrive there, just sit or lie in the wonders of the first level. (Yes, there are higher levels of it.) When you arrive at the first level, you will find cat guides to take you to even higher levels. Some of you may enjoy the first level for a long, long time. There is nothing right or wrong here, so just follow your heart path. It will always lead you wisely. Or as the cats say… walk straight ahead, and follow your heart to the right path.

Once you arrive at the first level, you are ready to tune into some practical guides to understanding elegance. They are freely given… You will know when you are ready, you will not need to ask. Remember, do not go on a moment before. If your heart is not in the right place, it will not work.

If you are ready, enter…

Let's begin with something simple like shopping for that which expresses the inner you. Once you are in the right space, and know who you really are… you can find clothes and gems anywhere. They will simply materialize, often even as gifts. You can find treasures in boutiques, and second-hand stores, or even just sifting through your closet. It does not require many items or much cost. Just seek out vibrancy with a light heart, and it will find you.

If ever you feel in need of extra help, just contact Crystal of montessoricats.com or text her at 954.801.8277 and she will set you up with a healer kitten. Just tell her

Gemini sent you directly, and she will understand. If you are really lucky, you will get one of Gemini's kittens… however, that happens only every two years.

You can begin your search like a calico… but it may be easier to begin with tabby, with grey or browns of silvery stripes and spots. They say tabby cats were actually named after an ancient batik pattern from the old world marketplaces along the silk roads. You can never go wrong emulating tabby. Or sheer blacks… They say a woman with a black cat can do anything… but that is another story entirely. Qwilleran's *Haunting tails*. It is a bit mysterious and a book to be read after midnight. Check out Qwill's picture on Montessori Cats website. A woman or man in black speaks of elegance and mystery.

Now is the fun part. Explore yourself in new ways. Try a tailored plush suit if you are accustomed to a more casual style. If you are a man of blue and grey limits, try a pink shirt. Try something new, once a week. If you like tight jeans, wear a flowing kimono. Crystal often has her nails painted in pink and grey swirls to match Collette's unique paws. Collette can be seen on Montessori Cats website. She is also working on a book of her own on the sacred nine, past lives for people and their cats, called *Remembering Together*.

Hats, scarfs, ties, barrettes even veils—all accessories of any shape and size—do wonders for self-expression. Always find new treasures and pass along old ones. Elegance is a flowing stream of inspiration, not a stagnant lake. It is living with a quiet grace and expanding vibrations, all at the same time. It's expressing your deepest self, and evolving like a snake skin. It's mindfulness, with an orchestra, or a band… or just singing out loud with your soul's song.

Remember, do not try to follow the guides in a literal sense. Just allow them to drift into your unconscious spaces, and they will do their magic in your sleep or when you are not paying attention.

Now, let us continue. Read on… It is always important to be clean. You are never too old or macho to go to a spa. If you like, go often. You can always bring the spa home with flowers and herbs like roses, lavender and eucalyptus leaves… or put essential oils in a tub, and soak in the light of the moon or a candle. We cats think creating a spa ambiance in your home is actually much better than going to the spa. However, it will help most people to explore a spa at first for inspiration. For right now… get up and drink fresh fruits in water. Never citrus. Never, ever citrus. We cats prefer you to indulge in the gentler fruits and herbs… grapes, watermelon, berries, mugwort, cat nip etc.

By now, some of you may have suspected that this book is being channeled to our friend Crystal who is half cat and half person from our cat point of few. There are very few like her, living in both the cat and person world. We have much to teach you through her voice. We love you, but despair watching you muddle through your life. We have so very much to guide you through and can enlighten your life into a vivid happiness… to live life with serenity and a secret smile

Allow yourself, to allow your imagination free range, flowing… peacock style.

Before We Continue…

Let's go back to creating the home spa. It is all about pampering… Pamper yourself, or another, or two or four kittens. Sit outside on a beach, in the sunshine… sipping watermelon water. Eat an entire can of tuna or caviar or smoked oysters or dehydrated crunchy red pepper seaweed. Stretch out in the moonlight or climb into an amethyst cave. Create a salt room with Himalayan salt lamps. You can nap half and half or go drink half and half. Half imagination, half real world. Half home spa. Half outer spa. On occasion indulge in a spa manicure, or pedicure… and sharpen your claws often, or file them if you prefer. Color them or massage them into a creamy glow. Indulgence is personal, as Cashmere likes to point out. He is rather insistent on being indulged.

Gemini says, the main concern is that you begin to use your imagination and explore so you can create… what your inner being needs, for a roaring purr. The more you invite your imagination to grow, the more it will expand. It's really that simple. In essence, just listen to your cat, purr more… and watch what happens.

If you get stuck, take a break or a trip to Jamaica for a change of scenery. Or even better… Cat Island in the

Caribbean. It's not really necessary, but changes of the environment seem to help people. We cats just change positions. Try both. You may be surprised where this practice leads you to. While nature and all natural settings are always a wonder, full of chirping birds and crickets… there are also some tasty mice to be found in city alley ways if you are in the know.

When you learn to change positions, perspectives can change in a flash. We cats see the world more like a diamond cut into many dimensions of sparkle and fire. We are far sighted and some of us can see into the next dimension… into the worlds of ghosts and spirits. It is really not that hard to do if you want to try to be clairvoyant. There is an entire chapter of it, in Collette's book. Some of the cats can see even further… into the future, or alternative realities as we call them. There are also alien universes, that are all commonly available to most cats. Many of you are actually equally farsighted, if you wish to explore the pathways. However, we are going too far ahead for our purposes here and now.

Let's begin slowly, with patience…

Remember, the important thing now is not to get overwhelmed or concerned about doing anything. Just allow the new ways of being to flow into you, and be absorbed by this magic potion. It is both powerful and empowering. The main thing here, is to begin to begin, to learn to change perspectives in a blink by a blink. This leads us to share our secret blink meditation. Try it!

The Blink Meditation

Arrange yourself on a very soft pillow, or a clean litter box or dirty laundry as you prefer, and close your eyes.

Stretch out your muscles so you are as tall or as long as possible.

Relax and curl up into a semicircle or just hang loose.

Imagine a soft purr in your heart.

Really hear it vibrate your heart.

Allow it to vibrate louder and feel the purr vibration grow bigger, and envelop your whole body and any cats cuddling up.

Imagine the purr running up and down your spine and out through your tail.

Take a deep breath and enjoy the vibration.

Allow the purr vibration to get smaller and just surround your heart.

Send it to all your cats, and allow the purr to go back and forth between you and your cat or cats. Feel the connections grow. Listen for secret messages, they will come… after a little practice.

Return the purr to just surround your heart, and let it flow once again around your body with a shimmering brilliant light.

Open up your eyes, as you allow the purr vibration to soften, and fade.

Take several deep breaths and stretch out slowly and fully from head to tail.

When you are finished… eat a cookie, a sardine, and drink a cool water or some coconut water… whatever you prefer. Some people drink Scotch, but we do not advise it. A word here about intoxicants, that are not necessary. They tend to slow down the process. However, there are no absolute rules, ever… so listen to your heart. And read on…

This is a great meditation to play with. Try it and see. It is a great way to end or begin a nap, anytime. You can practice early morning, or midnight. As I said, there are no absolute rules. You can even try the practice with another sensitive person, after you have been at it for a while with your cat friends.

Let's talk about feathers a little. Feathers, as we have often said, cannot be underestimated in their importance to life and happiness. Colorful or pale, long or short, they add elegance and beauty and joy. Peacock feathers are our great favorites. We suggest wearing a peacock feather hidden somewhere on you. We have heard it also has an aphrodisiac effect on people, FYI. More important, if you come across a stray and want to make friends with a cat you are smitten with… it's an excellent pick up toy. If discreetly hidden in a sleeve, or a pocket… a peacock feather can make you feel more confident, occasionally inspiring a cocky stance with other people. Hurrah for peacocks!

(You can try this with a rooster feather if you are very secure.)

Some people can play with this wearing a hat when they leave the house with a feather... from ostrich to chickens. Do not laugh, chicken feathers are actually quite lovely and fluffy, and smell divine. There are also lovely fake feathers for those who are tender hearted towards the birds.

A word about fake feathers, fun is fun. We cats love tender hearted people. Enjoy them all... although the real ones are closer to our hearts... Keep an open mind, and experiment with color and texture. Remember this can be real or imaginary so anything goes. Stay away from eagles and blue jays; even in the imaginary world they can be a bit fresh.

Some Persians have lost much of their sense of smell. They still adore feathers, and really enjoy having a feather lightly touching up and down their spine, and through their fur... Try it! There is always a creative way around any limitation. That is a subtle but important key to remember.

There is a legend of one extremely creative person who wore a belly dance costume made of feathers, and danced for her cats. They enjoyed it immensely when she was younger. Elegance is also about aging with grace. Now that same person carries feather fans to play with her cats who still adore her efforts to please.

It's cute to have a smudge on your face as a kitten. As an adult, do wash it off or get a facial. Use a sandpaper cream to clean well and glow. It's adorable as a kitten to have a fluffy loose knot. As an adult it can lead to some extreme issues, like getting a lion cut, haircut. Even worse is a bath, that comes with tidal waves and tornado dryers. Age gracefully, and avoid these situations altogether.

Crystal has read of a cat groomers association, that teaches gentle cat grooming. She wants to go to South Carolina, with Earl Grey to study it. Dave is not too excited about it. Earl Grey is even less enthusiastic. Earl Grey is a long hair Scottish fold at Montessori Cats who tends to hold onto poop under his tail. It's not very attractive even to the girls in heat. Let the small shit go, as they say… into the litter boxes.

The message here is don't act like a kitten when you are a cat. Be who you are, and you will be free. Age with grace, agility and dignity. Keep your head high on your shoulders and leap, with grace. Blink slowly with deliberate elegance. Old whiskers are often popular as fortune tellers. You may not have everyone laughing to tears by flipping antics, but is that what you really want as an adult cat. Being elegant is about knowing how to be cool. Stache, Qwill's mom, could jump at ten, very high over a bed and could land delicately like she was flying. She really knew how to be cool.

Just absorb these messages, and take a nap. Or put a deposit down on a Montessori kitten, and get your life back on track if you are really lost. It's OK if you are journeying like a kitten, missing the prey. It takes time and practice to find elegance. Plant these seeds of wisdom to develop an elegant attitude. Walk softly, on velvet paws… and keep an open purr…

It's all out there—everything you need to be elegant. Even better, most of the tools are free for all who know how to seek. Practice the purr meditation before you read the next guides, and by the end of this book… you will have mastered Tortitude. Always remember It can really help to get a tortoiseshell cat, oh it can help.

(One day a woman with a tortoiseshell cat will run for president. There is a legend, that when a tortoiseshell cat lives in the White House, the country will prosper… I know there are the folks who say the legend is about a Sphinx cat… but only time will tell so let us agree to disagree without a hiss.)

Be notorious. Everyone loves a cat mystery story. Just be certain there are no police around listening if there are any cat bunglers involved. Create a mystique around you, especially in the past… Grandparents who come from Scotland, an exotic name or tale or tail. We knew a cat who often spoke of her grandmother Hext. She descended from Salem, Mass and was a witch's cat. Who knows? She always did seem to disappear on full moons. She named her first daughter Magic, and her second daughter Charm. She went to a cat show and won ribbons in household pets as a straight ear Scottish Fold. She developed a real legend of glamour and magic. She was truly elegant.

You can reinvent yourself! You can... reinvent yourself!

Glamour cannot be overlooked. Use lots of it, in ribbons and gems... and even an occasional sequin. Crystal sometimes puts a diamond like bracelet on Collette like a collar. It's safe and stretches as it sparkles. When Collette has it on, both cats and people step aside... Although glamour is often seen surrounding gems, it is really more about the sparkle and sparks of life. Rolled up aluminum balls make great sparkle toys. Diamond earrings are glamorous, but so are glass cut mosaics.

It all works, as glamour is not a physical object... it is an energy. You cannot touch it, it is a like a magic spell... causing the very air to shimmer and glow. All masks have glamour and mystery flowing out of them. If you don't understand glamour, put on a mask and look at yourself in the mirror for twenty minutes. Then take it off, and look at yourself differently. There you are, at another angle. You may need to try it a few times to take it seriously, and transcend... If you don't give up it is quite an adventure. Having a glass of cat catnip tea or Kahlua and cream, hold the Kailua... can also be helpful. You can also try looking deeply into your cat friend's eyes, and blink slowly. Then look into a mirror... lazily. Visions will follow the dedicated.

One can also get glamorous taking a bath in organic rose petals, or oils. Peach, pink, purple or red are best during a new moon or a night with lots of winds. Silk or cashmere robes, and silk and velvet slippers also assist well in these glamorous adventures. You will get inspired, and carry on...

Music creates moods and elegance, as you may be starting to see, is a fragile... rather ethereal mood. If it were a color, I would call it eggplant black. In music it can be anything... a saxophone, or harp, Spanish guitar, rock, drum circles, rap... Both music and elegance have many ways that lead one to enchantment. It's really all about finding your inner purr, rhythm and pouncing. We like both music that soothes and powerful rhythms that hypnotize... to melt worries, release fears, to melt and transform the ordinary into the extraordinary.

Think of it this way... elegance is like a spider's web... very delicate and fragile looking, but powerful enough to trap the bugs of life, and create beautiful weavings. It can never hurt to open up and expand your surroundings. Re-invent your bedroom with silk pillowcases, that keep your fur smooth... or find plush carpets that become a chrysalis of transformation each morning as you pounce out of your dreams.

Everyone can create elegance. Even an old cat who can no longer pounce has the glamour of the ancients. Our memories create enchanting stories and legends. Shared experiences and dreams link hearts together. Story telling is an art... Sometimes the memories of the past are better than when we lived them. Being dramatic is another often overlooked part of elegance. I'm not talking about cat show drama. The show of movie star glamour is only one type of drama. There is a quiet everyday drama, like disappearing to get attention... Try taking a walk out the back door without telling anyone you are leaving, then just return. Experiment with drama. Disappear one day, hiss the next, and purr with all your heart in between. Life is a glorious adventure.

Elegance is like that... the mystery of flowing change. It's serendipity and caprice and illusion and charm. Chase it, it's a delight to pounce on but you will never capture it. You can create unique ways of your own to tame it temporarily, for yourself.

1)

Elegance
Cannot be captured
It is like an unknown perfume
You remember from a dream
On a beautiful friend
You will meet
Two hundred years in the future
Or remember from a past life

Cats walk with it
With their everyday stride
Some people
Understand its magic
And ignite its power
Wearing an aura
Of veils and velvets
Leathers and silks
And are adored

You can develop its secrets
By breathing
In the magic of the purr
And letting go
Of human manners
And limitations

Keeping company with felines
Invites it
Nobody owns its essence
It is a free spirit
And defies gravity
And age

It is one of the great
Art forms
Like sculpture,
Creating beauty and space
Out of mystery

2)

Pouncing
On velvet
Paws
Her everyday walk
Is a dance
She fills a room
Like cinnamon baking
And appears and dissolves
Like melting butter
To your tongue

She says her work
Is in business
And she is wordy
But her eyes
They hypnotize
And she's mostly
Unemployed
Without a reference

She sparkles
Like a star
In the night
And feels like a magnetic force
The diamond ring
Around a planet
Whirling

She wears half veils
She calls crochet
Like ornaments
Woven in her hair
And dropped on her
Like the crown
On a queen

She walks in beauty
And courts mystery
As her eyes close
Softly, she purrs
Secrets in her sleep

She is elegance
With today's funky twist
A long blue streak
In her black hair
Floating like a feather

She leaves a room
And her perfume
Floats behind her
Like a magic cape
Or a drum
In the distance
On a sultry night

Guide 2

On being still

"People are a lot like feathers, they come and go with the next wind." I had become accustomed to Gemini's words to her best friends. I would often eavesdrop on the whispers. "Don't get too attached," she would often murmur to Pit Bull, a calico girl cat friend renowned for her extremely strong protective instincts towards her kittens. She was also a very good friend of Gemini, more like a sister. They had the same father, Beanie Baby the Great.

Gemini is a short plush coat Scottish fold tortoiseshell cat from Montessori Cat's Scottish Fold Cattery in South Florida. Plush coats are like velvet to touch, and she is no exception.

She is right now curling up on a book of Eastern Buddhist philosophy or it may be poetry, as I write. She was until recently a free spirit of a cat, enjoying life… just pouncing along… That was until recently, when her first son, Charles Dickens, was born on New Year's Eve… quite close to midnight.

It does seem that nothing in life is absolute. All philosophies and opinions are subject to change with experiences. Gemini's face is two colors... chocolate brown and golden orange. As a result, she has a very open mind. She is also the main writer who was inspired to begin this book. A few other voices, have joined in as we go along...

That brings us back to the purr meditation. We hope you have been practicing a few sessions by now. If not, that is fine... just begin. Every day is a new opportunity to pounce on life, never look back with regret. The purr meditation, is a wonderful tool for opening the mind to new adventures. Cats are very present tense. They may learn from yesterday, but today is the focus. If you are not inspired by the purr meditation, then don't do it. However, try it a few times first.

While you ponder that, here is as good a time as any to share some general words from the cats that I may have failed to mention. Do not ever underestimate the power of meditation, as well as naps.

With practice and a few guided visualizations, you can begin to create a better quality of life, with a more vital life force. Everyone desires that, and you can easily achieve it. Keep reading on, for more techniques. You are in, as they often say, the right place and at the right time, to be inspired. This secret is truly beyond anything else in this guide in terms of important first steps. It takes a blend of courage and practice, laziness and imagination... to start every day in a different way... to jump to new heights. It also takes a little patience and dedication, like hunting.

Just relax, and take a break... When you return, we will begin again. Beginning again, again is the key... For now, have a sardine, a plate of caviar and Champagne, and just open up your eyes... wider.

Look around you, noise and chaos are everywhere. It strains your nerves, drains your energy and exhausts you. You have to learn to step into another dimension to take breaks and escape to live at a slower vibration. To refresh your being, and slow down the aging process. That skill may not be quite as important as being a good hunter, we understand that all too well... but it is just as beneficial to life... maybe more. You can often find someone else to hunt for you... but only you can learn how to be still in your center. You will acquire remarkable improvement in your health and all your relationships if you spend time mastering this chapter almost immediately.

It is not as complicated as you may think, to stop... moving... and allow the world to rush around you. Some people start with yoga or Tai Chi, and that is a fine beginning. We cats love the ancient cultures of China and Tibet. We just have taken it a few steps further and simplified it a bit. Just stop moving, right where you are now. Watch. Listen... until you notice how all the world is made up of energy waves, connecting us all on some great invisible realm.

Once you begin to understand this, you can remain very still, with greater ease. You can begin to tune into the connections and experience life at a slower flowing pace. You can become a great hunter, a poet, or just enjoy life at a deeper level. Some people will not even notice anything has changed about you. Your cats will. They notice everything significant about you, within and without.

Being still is almost as simple as crossing the corner of a street. It is a shift, not in place but in space. Don't try to understand this logically... just read, and let the words sink in gradually like water, in a desert fountain.

At this more leisurely pace, your body can unwind and heal. You can think, without the pressures of everyday demanding you to focus and answer too many linear questions and concerns all at once.

Or at all... you don't have to be ready to begin. Just start. Be still, and listen... You may be surprised at the answers that come to you. You may even smile like a Cheshire cat, and feel no need to share in the secrets you discover. Some discoveries are deeper than words. You may find the need to talk less, and appear wise in a mysterious silence. You will for certain... become more present with your world. Instead of worrying about your work, you may start to notice the blue colors of the sky as they shift to the purple grey of twilight. You will feel more content, just watching the river flowing... It is amazing, and so simple.

To begin, please start taking five minute naps four times a day. Yes, just do it... and then we will expand slowly... close your eyes, for five minutes today. Try it! Later in the week, or on a quiet day... try ten, or even twenty. This is only one hour out of twenty-four. If you cannot do it all, well then do as much as you can, or think you can. I guarantee if you do it, you will be amazed at how much better you feel. Start with the five minutes, four times a day… Just breathing, and daydreaming.

Blink a few times to realign your senses. This is also a fine thing to explore right before a nap… Blinking is an important skill… Try slow blinking with your cat.

What is meant by a nap, exactly? It can be done in a few different ways.

It is closing your eyes, and going blank… and just letting go of everything… You can sit by a river and dream of another time. You can also just sit and have a drink, even a smoke or a glass of lemon water… Just close your eyes in your favorite chair, or on a bus on a long ride… or just about anywhere you happen to find yourself, you can lose yourself. It is taking a break from your thoughts and worries. It's a nap, meant to refresh.

It can realign the spirit. It creates a resilience in your body and soul. It is not to be done rigidly. This is a free flowing experiment for you. You can just sit and read a book for five minutes or sing a song until you feel comfortable taking a break from ordinary reality. The key is to take a break. "What about my responsibilities?" you may say. "They will all still be there waiting for you, T…ry it…" Gemini says, with a blink.

To start we just want to get you used to becoming accustomed to taking a bit of time and putting it aside.

Then blink slowly, several long slow blinks... each time you begin.

That will help you to get into the right spirit.

By the way, if you are confused... remember that napping is altogether different than meditation. Meditation is more Yang, and napping is more Yin if you prefer to see it in those terms. If you are interested in exploring these concepts...We will leave that to the Balinese to explain more of that in their future book, *The Eastern Purr Triangle*...

Both meditation and napping are important, significant steps to enter the new ways of being we hope to cultivate within you. Meditation is like a mind exercise, Napping, the way we understand it to be, is making a decision to change directions. It is a choice, a time management exercise of sorts. Even a new mom can do it, if she is creative... flipping a tail leisurely, during nursing. You can have a drum circle with your kittens, or just cuddle up together. It is not so important what or how you do it... just start doing it. It's simple, to begin... five minutes, four times a day.

A cuddle nap is the most powerful nap imaginable. Energies bounce back and forth... Soft to hard, strong to weak... it both balances and revives all in the embrace. Now if you add a purring cat to the experience, it can become delirious. Crystal calls it twilight napping.

It seems to do wonders for her, although we have noticed that her clothes do suffer a bit in the process. Delirium seems to be a more important goal to her. It does require the trust and love of several cats. If you are so inclined, do try it.

We cats are not saying that you will no longer have the old human issues. You will still have to deal with them. It is only that by learning to be still, you will be more a part of life as a whole. More connected…When you join in, and connect in stillness… you naturally find your center. Then, when you do return to human activities… you will see things differently. You will have new perspectives, and will find yourself seeing new possibilities to solve your concerns. Don't strain to think, or try too hard… just invite yourself to be still. From your center you will sense the right roads to take, make better decisions and risks, like knowing when to climb a tree or whom to marry.

Sharper instincts will start to develop within… and you will just know things. Like when to take a risky gamble and raid the garbage, or when to hide under the bed 'til the storms pass. Sometimes you will find that you just need to climb a tree to get a different perspective. That can, under certain situations, be surprisingly helpful.

People get hung up in rushing, and thinking… worrying and more rushing. Try beginning by not rushing the morning. Be late for important obligations. Allow life to come to you. Be mysterious, like a cat. Gemini says she does this every day, for hours. Then she takes a bath… and does it all over again. Sometimes several times. She has taught these secrets to Charles Dickens, her first kitten. Now she is generously sharing it with you. Give it a try! Start by going for a really long slow walk to nowhere…

and see where it leads. Walking slowly... Really slowly. Slowing down is a most important step to filling life with Tortitude.

If you have reached this page, it is a very good sign. You have taken the first pounces...

Since words like these do have their limits... the cats are sending you a few poems... that will assist in bringing the words to a deeper level inside of you. Read them aloud, or in a whisper before a nap. Some things are more than they seem, as is true of the poetry.

They are more than words... the poems are enchantments within the guides. You can read them, rub your hands over them, or sleep with them under your pillow. It is all up to you, listen to your own inner guides.

They are starting to wake up. Listen!

1)

Breathe in silence, ever so slowly
And breathe out… with magnificence
Your inner light,
In a leap of faith…
There you will be guided,
Like the Cheshire cats of London
Into a new mysterious realm

Simply stop trying to attain a goal
And ramble with indifference…
And you will find a new path.
That is more vivid,
Then you could ever imagine…
Within your soul.

Without trying
Or rushing
The river flows
With great energy,
And no effort
There is great joy in the sparkles of life…
It holds a magic mirror
And a deep serenity
You too can find your way, if you follow along quietly…

2)

In the Mediterranean
They know how to live, better
sunshine bakes the air…
With the sweetness of lime blossoms,
And dreams drift
Over centuries… walking slowly
not knowing where… they are going
(or even caring)

There, the sea understands so much
And heals in shades of blue, flowing
As the tides come in
And goes out, again and again
And again…
In an endless dance,
While people rush to go nowhere, forgetting…
Where and why.
Birds soar, avoiding the earth
their wings, laughing

While cats and lovers just
Smile, lazily in the sunshine
Embracing the delights

3)

Once upon a time, on a New Year's Eve Gemini, a tortoiseshell cat… gave birth
to a cream colored fuzz
Named Charles, her first son,
In the middle of a dark pandemic

On that night…
Far away firecrackers exploded in the sky
People drank
And cried with greed, for their youth…
For gold, and lost gambles,
Missing the opportunity
Of the moment

Gemini's son
Brightened her days…
Into a glow, of wonder
And joy that just had to leap forward…
Cuddling closer and closer
Into his loving destiny, purring
Growing strong in the ways…
Of listening and watching,
Wisdom…
Hunting new games
Through him
Both light, and dust…
That transformed her

4)

This is a lullaby that Gemini sang to Charles

Be gentle with yourself
You are a song
Of the universe, sing
From your heart
And dance, with the floating steps of play
Leaping lightly, with the day

Curl in a little ball, of fur and purrs
Become so full of light, that your soul can
Drink deeply
Of the holy milk and honey
Daily life brings you
With a deep faith in good in all that is free

Know you can
Do anything, enchanted… the stars shine
For you every night
As we sit in the stillness
Of life
And in the glorious rush, of being alive
never hold your breath

Guide 3

On movement

Let's keep keeping it simple. Think about it, the only time your life really opened up is when you allowed yourself the discomfort of something new, and you stretched your everyday expectations to explore it. Much of the time it was not by choice. A crisis spun into your life, without warning… tornadoes, hurricanes, storms and fires are often nature's way of creating a change. People resist change, and are a bit like trees and rocks that way. We cats change with the wind… warm balmy winds are a delight for shedding coats… with long leisurely baths to follow. You can never take too many baths. Gemini says when you do not know what to do, start licking. Cold winds from the north help our coats to grow… lush whiskers and plush coats that are luxurious and cosy. Wind is good for the mind if you let it blow through your soul. It rips away at old cranky haunting thoughts that do need to be released every so often. Even cats, especially older ones who are like people, get a bit set in their ways. Winds blow away stagnation in all forms. Winds are alive, and depending on the direction… they have

Very different energies. South winds are carefree. North winds are cool and contemplative with an occasional temper tantrum. West winds are the experimenters, blowing you open to explore new realities. East winds are meditative and deep, sunk in wisdom... like a mama cat queen.

Winds are amazing to walk about in. It is a free seminar on change and letting go.

Gemini says people need to follow the wins in their neighborhoods, and open up to change. The next time you go out in the early morning, smell the air. Feel the wind... and travel where it takes you. It may be a short walk, or it may be a new way of looking at something you have been stuck on. Wind is the catalyst for changing the seasons, embrace it! The wind is old, but it never ages. It is a pure force. It is even wiser than the trees, and has much to teach you.

If you spend time listening to the wind your psychic ability may suddenly develop and astound you. It just takes a little time, and a little shift to follow.

Just be... free, free, free. Do not worry so much about money, people. Let your fears go and you will have all that you need. It is a secret, that nature is the great provider. Like rats, it blows in new opportunities for you, when you let go of all fear. Fear is the great blocker, of abundance. Fear is stagnant energy. Life was meant to be lived like the wind, flowing and magical.

Bravo, an old cat who lived many wise years once told Crystal the secret to his happiness. Bravo did not have an easy life, yet he was always happy… and open to life. As a kitten he got lost from his princess girl who loved him madly. He went for a walk one day, and the trees seemed to tangle up and confuse him. He tried and tried but could not find his way home. Starving and even shot by a pellet gun, he begged for food in desperation.

He was rescued by a kind couple who planned to get him better and then take him to the pound, as it was called in those old days. He lived for many weeks in their washer room, as they had two Siamese cats who were quite prejudiced towards other breeds. Bravo could have become bitter but he never did. He turned his heart to love and new opportunities. He purred, he bumped heads into the ankles of his people friends… and soon he was in both their laps.

It did not take long, and they were captured by his charms, and decided they needed to find hm a special home. The new home was with a woman named Betsy. She was an old hippy who loved him dearly for many, many years. Crystal has a strong feeling they hang out together in heaven as she writes this.

Now Betsy was a bit of a free spirit herself, and allowed Bravo to run outside at night, climbing trees. He could climb a palm ten feet high in a minute, and he hunted like a tiger. One day some cruel boys kicked him, crushing his right rear leg. Bravo survived, but he was badly injured. He managed to limp home. He still did not become bitter, and kept his heart open to love. Betsy was getting old and sick, and could not take care of him any more.

She worried and complained to her friend Crystal that she did not know what to do for him. Crystal flew him from Florida to New Jersey, where he received both medical care such as traditional surgery… and acupuncture, PT and massage. Brave healed and thrived. He kept his leg, and he opened his heart to his new family… He continued to fall in love with new people, that he inspired and was inspired by… for many long, happy years. Crystal still misses him, as nobody could purr quite like Bravo.

He ended up living back in Florida with Crystal and Dave, her new husband in the Montessori Cats Cattery. He died one night, a very old cat, looking out of a large window over the river, remembering all the many people he had been graced to love, and be loved by.

Bravo's secret was he kept an open heart to new adventures, and was very present tense. Even when he was deeply hurt, he never gave up on life. He watched for the new winds of change. Winds can help you bring in a change if you allow yourself to wander in them. Even in the darkest days… You can trust the winds to bring in something new and wonderful.

If you believe in life and change, like Bravo you will have a long and happy life. It will not always be easy to stretch and change… but it will be magnificent. There will be some challenges that are still tough. Bravo did not like acupuncture at first, but he loved the way he felt after a treatment. He allowed himself to follow the winds that swept through his life. He trusted life.

Take up exercise and move and stretch. The physical and mental… the body, mind and soul need to be balanced. You must stretch in every direction every day to be fully alive in life. Reach out…

Even in the spiritual level, stretching is important… Growth keeps a soul vibrant and sensitive to both new and old ideas. We once knew a kitten who fell asleep on a book on reincarnation, and had a dream she was back in ancient Egypt in the good old days… when cats were worshipped as gods. She had a lot to say from her dreams. Some of the cats at Montessori who liked to do a bit of catnip, thought she was very enlightened. Her name is Confection, and she has presence as well as a beautiful white coat.

A word about catnip and herbs. A little bit here and there can help a cat to wake up and open up… too much can leave them dehydrated and tired. A little whipped cream on party night, or a special occasion with others you love is fine fun. Too much of it makes one fat and sluggish. Moderation and balance is the key here.

If you keep moving your body, mind and spirit there is no telling where you will go. Qwilleran tells the cats a story that he once went to Ohio to learn cat massage with Crystal on a horse farm when he was a kitten. Right, kid, some of the older cats said to hm as though there was no such thing. You are over stretching your kitten imagination, something kittens do tend to do. The truth is it really did happen. There are more magical experiences in the universe than you may imagine.

Do not forget to stretch in between your exercising… along with naps and cuddles. Cuddle often in between adventures. Moderation and balance is the key. That is one of Gemini's favorite sentences. She wanted Crystal to write it seven times in this chapter alone… but decided it was a bit excessive. Since we were mentioning naps, and stretching… I might add that dreaming is often a restorative stretch into another realm. Go with the flow…

Life welcomes you
Whether your nose is pink or black
Or in between
May you enjoy many treats
And much gravy
In the moonlight

If you move
Your body and soul freely
You will have many secret adventures
And much fun
Even long soulful cuddles
That can lead to true love

May you live a long life
Like the legendary cat named Magic
Of many stripes and spots on her belly
Who was so old
She forgot her birthday.

Go with the flow
Of life
Like the wind spins
Flying through the air
In spring
Like a kitten running sideways
With the joy
Of charging life

When you live
Stretching and dancing
Through the wild journeys
Of life your paw prints
Will never gather
Dust
On a stagnant windowsill
From worry

Guide 4

A guide to the Benefits of Adventure and Joy

It is a fine thing to be still, to listen to the soul… and curl up on a soft pillow. When one is in doubt as to what to do it is a wise pathway. Like all good things in life, there must be a balance with stillness and motion. That is the secret that keeps one growing. Ask any kitten, and they will purr… When stillness and movement are mastered, and do take your time with this. A week, a year, a life, or two… whatever it takes, then we can move on… to the next guide…

Adventure, that leads to joy!

Whether you are like a kitten getting out of the birthing box, or a lion coming out of the den…

After resting and stretching, one can move forward into the land of adventure. Adventure is a journey and it is much more… It is a state of mind. It is magic. It is opening one's heart to what is new, and saying yes. Again and again, yes… It is bowing to the unknown with honor. We will as always simplify things for you. It can begin with getting your passport, or some traveling papers from the vet ten days before your journey. I hope you all are in the process of getting your passport updated, or dusted off from the back of the drawer this week. It is simple enough, and such profound gestures have interesting echoes...

If you have not already done so, please begin...

You do not have to go very far to find adventure. You can climb a new tree, or try a new recipe for gravy. There are many, many opportunities in this world. Gemini suggests you might want to visit the pyramids in Cairo, but she is a bit impatient at times. Certainly a trip to the pyramids would give you a jump start, but it is not necessary to start out that way. You can visit a museum full of Egyptian mummies... and listen to their secrets in the dark, or learn to read hieroglyphics on Zoom. Ancient Egyptians worshipped cats as gods, so they are a practical place to begin. Some adventures take an hour, others a week, and some a life time, or two... Crystal started collecting ancient coins. Of late she is spending some time listening to music from the Middle Ages. Dave told me he was going to buy her a harpsichord for Christmas.

Even though he does not have the historical periods of the music perfectly in rhyme with time... Dave understands the spirit of adventure, more than most. He and Crystal do have a great advantage, as they have lived with Gemini since she was born.

The first adventure Gemini suggests you go on is an airplane to Florida to get a new kitten from Montessori Cats. You might want to stay a few nights by the sea in Miami. The water is warm and blue and balmy... and the sunshine will help you loosen up. After a few nights, and night caps... you can return home, with a kitten who will help lighten your way.

Just understand that one adventure leads to another, and one kitten can sometime lead to several cats. Adventures and life cannot always be contained... but you have been warned. Gemini says it is worth the risks.

Once you begin to open your spirit to adventure, there is no map telling where it may take you. As Gemini is fond of saying... People are like feathers, they blow with the wind. There is a little island in the Caribbean called Cat Island, Gemini also recommends. Although any of the Caribbean islands, can be quite helpful with stubborn cases. They are off the mainland, and give one a little more perspective. You can also read a few travel books. We advise you to travel with friends. To go off, with a pride of companions... or at least one other. You can also carry your cat friend on a plane with that special certificate from your vet. Cats have flown to Paris, even Japan. They do prefer first class if you can arrange it.

We know of a cat flying to San Francisco from Atlanta... who got out of her carrying case in flight... while her person was sleeping. She was eventually found sitting with contentment in the lap of an elegant lady in first class, who was rather reluctant to let her go. *Cela se voit.*

If you are on a budget, you might just visit a close by city, and roam about. There are always new sites to see, gardens to visit... and bugs to be enchanted by. Crystal likes to collect jade… and has been traveling to gemology exhibits when they are in different cities. She tries to explore the town for a day, whenever she visits somewhere new. Although you don't have to search for Ethiopian restaurants, as she does… even a hot coffee, in a new café can lead to interesting discoveries. Hunger and thirst are great motivators for adventure, so keep food in your mind.

Also mice.

Speaking of food, it is always a good idea to feed your cat a new and tasty treat now and then. Shrimp in a bowl, is a powerful wake up call. Or even a dish of pure homemade gravy, straight up… hold the salt. Not every adventure will work out, and that's OK. Crystal once brought some mouse cans of cat food home from a cat show, and it was positively disgusting. Several of the cats threw up immediately… just upon opening the can. That being said… we suggest you taste new foods, in the spirit of adventure… even if you do throw up, now and then. Gemini says it cleans out the digestion.

Dave likes to smoke grass, the cats like to eat grass, and Crystal likes to grow grass. We are a grass centered family. Be open to exploring weeds, and herbs and spices. Anything new will open up your senses in ways that you cannot imagine. It is not so much what you do. It is being open to life, with the spirit of the wind. I cannot stress enough how good it is to eat a little grass, and blow your fur in the wind, by an open window… in the sunshine. Wind and sunshine are like spices for planning a new adventure.

If you cannot think of anything new, try changing directions from north to south, or east to west. Such subtle shifts can actually be quite helpful…

Although travel is one way to have adventures, there are many more. If you are on a budget, you might try collecting kaleidoscopes. There are even craft schools, that have workshops in how to build them. Some people really get lost in the colors, like a cat toy. Another suggestion is telescopes, that can open up the universe to you. You can visit a planetarium to try one out. The purpose of such journeys is to expand your vision from the mundane to the magical. Cats see magic everywhere. There is no reason you cannot, you just may need a little help. These are just suggestions, your adventures are your own. Private. Between you and your cat.

Many cats love to climb trees, for perspective. We cats think people can get some of the same clear views climbing mountains. If you climb to the top of a mountain, and camp out in the moonlight… you will never regret it. You can begin with a hiking group… or you can learn to ski. If nobody is looking, you might even try to climb a tree. At the very least, try walking about with a pair of binoculars, to watch the birds. It is quite exhilarating, with a chicken sandwich. This might even lead to you becoming a private detective, or witnessing a murder.

The best thing about adventure is that it takes you out of yourself, and your ordinary life. People are just too self-absorbed. As adults they become too one dimensional, and trapped within their routines. Adventures are the key to opening an inner freedom that cats never lose touch with. This leads to joy... Joy is a generous by product of adventure. It can also be jump started with a purr. So once again, keep a cat by your side. Once you bond, most cats will share with you most generously as they have much joy in abundance.

For those of you with a metaphysical bend, you can try inner adventures on magic carpets or Tarot cards. Your cat will be happy to help you with such pursuits. There are many decks to choose from, and you can explore for hours, or during your lunch hour. You will return from lunch with a curious appetite for life. Ignite your secret self, and follow your curiosities.

They will lead you to some amazing adventures. There are no rules to adventures. I repeat, there are no rules to adventures.

You may enjoy art, and take a class to learn to sketch your cat. They make beautiful models.

We know a man, who became a great sculpture, and is now in public exhibits. He began with clay sculptures of his cat. He still makes her some fancy bowls, that he carves out of stone. It is a good thing to thank your muse. As often, and as many ways as you can. Gemini says chicken of the sea, is a good start... but she also enjoys jewelry, and gold collars.

Just doing something different, and out of the ordinary can open up the mysterious aspects of life. Walking in the moonlight, by a flowing river, when the snow begins to fall... simple things. Light a fire, or a candle... groom your cat, with a soft brush if you need more inspiration.

You are never really lost, with a cat by your side. Qwilleran says a woman, with a black cat... can do anything. Gemini tilts her head, at that... holding out some hope to men.

Life is a magical adventure, and when you open up your eyes and blink... the universe is yours to play with. Enjoy the journey!

If you are feeling a little lost as to where to begin, just be with your cat.

And follow along... Being open to adventure, with a cat by your side... will just bring it along naturally, so no worry... Kittens glow with joy, and remember, two kittens are even better than one! And twice as joyous. Joy flows, it is something you cannot capture or buy. Once it is yours, you can breathe and grow it Within you, even spread it around... wherever you go. That is nice. It is much appreciated and a rare treasure. The best things in life really are freely given by your cat.

Joy grows with a smile, and is nourished by laughing. It tastes like whipped cream or a kiss, or tuna. You can find it just about everywhere when you know what to look for.

If you play with your cat, every day... she will lead you to it, gently, and all the universe, with its secrets will be yours to know. We cats hope you share it wisely.

Or perhaps this is all simpler to understand in a poem.

Adventures
To inspire
Ricochet
In the moonlight
If you can be still
Enough to listen
With the widening
Of your heart

Inspired by feline
Myths and legends
Woven from ancient shadows
And dreams
Let your cat
Lead the way to wonders
She is both invisible
Yet frequently
Seen

If you take your time
With timing
As all cats do know
You can melt your human limits
Just try, to take it slow
As your cat laps up her whipped cream
From a sparkling silver bowl

Guide 5

The Guide on Caprice and Charm

Caprice started Montessori Cats Cattery with Dave at her side, a cattery of elegance and legendary beauty… which evolved out of a simple cat rescue. They were really rescuing love, sustaining and restoring love. That was many, many, years and lives ago. Once they realized what was truly going on, the cattery was born with a rapid transformation.

Caprice now watches over us lovingly, haunting the cattery with her endless charms and light. Only yesterday she smashed a metal sign on a dresser, that said dull women have clean homes. It almost knocked Crystal over when she was pleasantly vacuuming the paintings on the ceiling. Crystal smiled, and understood only too well, the message.

Caprice did not pay attention to the ordinary in reality when she was alive. She did not like limits or boundaries. She soared in her imagination, and she was an artist. She carried everyone she talked to with her. She did not bother with how limited things were. She listened deeply to people's souls and she saw what they were capable of becoming. She opened up windows that had been closed with rust and heartache.

Caprice used spray paint to open up possibilities. She colored life with a magic that was larger than life. Or maybe it was just that she understood more than the average person what was really important in life. Maybe it was that she had the advantage of the cats.

Caprice oozed charm. She was beautiful in youth, very exotic with a long dark coat of long hair. She always had cats by her side, many cats. This is, my dear readers, the number one rule of charm. Have a cat by your side. Or two or four, as Caprice would say. She lived like a cat, and knew all the cat secrets which she would use and share in her human form. I often wonder if she is reincarnated in one of Montessori's cats, in folded or straight ear. Many people have named their cat after Caprice.

Caprice listened to people's souls and ignored the rest. As a result, everyone felt she understood them. She listened, like a cat… It is, after all, rather simple, it's a matter of caring to pay attention. Caprice could command attention in a room or over the phone. She glowed, and her voice was raspy, like a cat's tongue. She spoke with deep conviction, or she did not speak at all. The heart of charm is just being present, and attentive to the small details of life. Life a mouse, running in the wall. Anyone can do that, just by slowing down their focus of attention. Even you!

Caprice was mysterious, and vibrant. She saw magnificence and wonder everywhere. She was also the bravest woman in the world. Before she died, she battled pain, with a divine grace… still loving, and embracing all who knew her in her charming presence She is deeply missed in her human form by all of us.

Caprice
Lives on
Like a sprite
In the garden
Dancing in the moonlight
Wearing a dazzlingly colored leaf dress
Agreeing to nothing
In the sun's forecast
Of reason

Caprice
Loves on
Dancing in our shadows
The way the dearly beloved do
Wearing wings
Like blue butterflies, that are rarely seen
Coming out of pale cocoons
Into the invisible mist of mystery

Her gentle smile
Could light up a soul
With a blink
Turning bitter into sweet
She danced the Earth
With a charm
That was pure
With the brilliance of a diamond's
Shine

You can never forget
The ones you lose
She used to say…
(and we never have)
But you can
Fall in love
Again.
(And again)

And so she lives on
Lovingly visiting
And haunting us
With her charms
And a long line
Of cats
With a healing presence

Guide 6

On Pouncing and Dancing and Finding your Inner Purr

Ah! When to pounce and when not to pounce. Now that is a question worth pondering. Where is Dave with the water gun? Look about, and be sensitive to your environment. Don't be like a kitten with an older cat, a nightmare to run away from. We have all seen it. Be real, if you cannot control your pounce, all the charm in the world will be useless. You will seem to others as an insufferable car salesman or a crazy kitten.

Don't pounce when someone is napping, cat or person. Naps are of great importance to the restoration of a being. Nobody wants to be pounced on during a precious nap. It is vulgar…Think about it, and be honest, Are you an insensitive pouncer? Sensitivity is the key here.

That being said, there are wonderful ways and times to pounce. Pounce lovingly when those you love come home, after an adventure. It dissolves the negative energy they may have picked up from the outside world. It also creates a positive flow in the home. It wakes up those you love, to the hunt in life. Pouncing is really a focus of attention. It can be given in the form of a hug or hello. Or a little leap forward, with a bump on the forehead.

Pouncing is all about timing… finding the right time and place to begin or end a romance, a hunt or a fight. The more you tune in to yourself, which will happen naturally as you read the guides, the more you will pounce at the right time and place.

Many people and kittens practice pouncing to the left, then pouncing to the right before they get it straight. Gemini says to please consider practicing on a curb or a chair first. There are no set rules about pouncing in life except one.

Don't be afraid to pounce if you feel it is right. Fear and hesitation are not a part of pouncing. Sensitivity yes, but never fear… just pounce. You may not always be right, but you will develop your intuition and become brave enough to pounce in life. In love… Over time, with much practice… It is a certain pathway to success.

Pouncing leads to dancing. Yes, cats dance! When you are not looking, they run sideways, to a secret rhythm. They fly across the room when no one is looking, calling it sky dancing. They leap when they feel confident. Give it a try!

People… Please dance as many ways as you can. Dance as often as you like.

Don't limit yourself. Be freestyle and just dance when you hear music that inspires you, even as you feed your cats. You do have more than one, I hope. Dancing is a spirit gift, that inspires your soul.

You can never pounce, or dance too often, if you are sensitive to others and guided by your heart. Life is fragile and short. Be as alive as you can as you live. It's a beautiful life. All nine of them...

"To err is human, to purr divine." Nothing could be more sweet to anyone than a passionate rambling purr.... except perhaps a soothing and sweet purr. There are many types of purrs, and they are all glorious... no matter how soft or loud they vibrate.

Purring soothes the soul, heals the body and the mind. Kittens are born and immediately wrapped up in their mother's purr. Cats purr when they fall in love, have a delicious meal., or when they cuddle up with an old friend. They purr to express the emotions that are beyond words like true love.

And yummy ecstasy.

They also purr to cheer up a buddy in pain, or one who is sick... or in transition. They purr to soothe themselves in loving self-care. It is like a central nervous system elixir that flows into the body-mind connection, and heals.

Purring is an ancient healing sound, that goes way back. Before the pyramids, where they knew that purrs could reach deep into the soul and heart. Purrs are the essence of a deep and healing intimacy. When you hear a purr you know you can go deep, and let go.

Some cats teach their people to purr. Crystal gets regular lessons. If you are really lucky, and attentive to your cats... it may happen to you. It's a sure sign you are on the right track in life. Be sure to keep any of the secrets to purring that your cat teaches you in confidence. Trust is important. Everyone hates a tattle tale.

Purring is close to music, and a form of sound healing. Many cats just adore music and will adjust the direction of their fur accordingly. That speaks volumes… Soft sounding music is a good place to begin exploring with your cats. Flutes, harps, the gentle jazz piano are sounds that soothe and are appreciated by many cats. Although not all!

Some cats like the thump of an organ. Others like the flutter of a mandolin, a bit close to a purr…. some say. Cats are individuals like people. They are influenced by their environment. If they are brought up with rock or rap as a kitten… there is just no telling, what they will enjoy.

All of Dave's cats love rock and roll, while Crystal's love the harp. That being said… Montessori cats really love their music. All music, from orchestras to fold songs. Generally cats' nervous systems are wired to softer sounds and harmonies. So when you first meet a new cat friend start out with the softer sounds and rhythms and explore…

Music and purrs are healing sounds. Being close to your cat's purr when you are sick is a potent medicine. Linger in it as long and as often as you can. Most cats are generous with their gifts if loved by you. Some of them are special healers, and they live to share it.

Spend some time every day enveloped or playing music. It is the path to finding your inner purr. Listen as much as you can, Gemini says… when you are driving or relaxing in a bath…just be with the music. Linger as long and as often as possible with songs. It is one of the great gifts of life. It's simple and free! It will spread what life is really about... being happy and sharing the joy... going beyond the hisses and hardships, and help you find your inner purr.

(Allow yourself to become enchanted, by your cat and by life itself.)

Purr is a great word. Just try saying it slowly. Like yoga's *ohm*... it has magic. It will keep you from growing old too fast, and may even turn back the clock a bit. It's free magic that was given to cats a long, long time... ago. Way back before recorded time. Like drumbeats in the desert that echo through the sands of time... there was a sacred secret rhythm, a hypnotic and mysterious sound. The purr, given as a gift, to the cats...

If you seek
Out, your inner purr… You will never find it.
Only knowing how
Not to look, will loosen it….
Getting really lost in loving pets Can lead you
to the secret
Of the sound
In the deep silences of your soul

What are you waiting for, a treasure hunt…
Is within everyone, for the reaching… With a chest
Of pure
Gold in the center of the mystery of you
Start, the hunting now…
With a canteen of melted ice cream
and a can of sardines packed for lunch in a backpack
Cat carrier
With your favorite kitten companion

There is no telling what you will find or what secret
You may decide to keep, hidden
Like your inner purr or outer peace
Or a fortune of lost Egyptian silver amulets
On a vacation in Cairo in the desert
Or even, at home
On a full moon in Pisces… On your favorite chair
Cuddling a tortoiseshell conjuring Tortitude
And Magic

Guide 7

The Original Purr

If a cat purrs
In your dreams
Allow the music
To inspire you
Like a rainbow
Rising out of the mists
And awaken
With a lighter heart

If a cat purrs
With your sadness
Know that a healer
Walks by your side
And you can trust The journey home
With a wise heart

If a cat purrs
By your presence
You can be certain
You have arrived
At true love
With a heart of gold

And you can enter
a magical realm
Where cats walk
In The silence between
The sounds and echoes
Like a rusty door
Opening up the secrets
Of the ages
With the Original Purr

When and if
You play
The music of your soul
(And an occasional ping pong)
For your cats
They will know
You understand
The mysterious inner realm
And there and then
The magic can begin

Guide 8

The guide to stretching and sleeping and the mysterious inner realms

To stretch is to be alive, when you stretch you open a pathway for life to flow. Freely, as it should. It is like a vitamin infusion. There is nothing healthier in the world than stretching. It releases tension, and unnecessary worries. It creates great flexibility in body mind and soul. People often stretch with yoga. which is a fine exercise. We have heard that many of the yoga exercises were patterned (possibly invented) by cats.

But cat stretching goes beyond yoga. To be effective stretching has to be a long hold and done very slowly with a bit of trembling at the end of the tail. This allows much emotional negativity and physical congestion to leak out into the mysterious ethers.

Stretching is to the body, what a smile is to your face. It transforms it. Watch your cat, and practice… without needing to be perfect. After all, you are not a cat, so we have lower expectations.

It is the perfect tonic after a nap. Nap is the extreme level of healing. Frequent naps are like frequent healings.

They help to balance the physical body and are essential to the well-being of cats. People would benefit from them immensely. Naps frequently disappear from people, after kindergarten… and only happen during a period of jet lag or illness. The happiest of people nap, and call it meditation. Whatever you call it, it helps one think clearly, dream and refresh the spirit, or plan a mouse hunt. It helps with all important things in life. A couple of doses of that a week does wonders for many nervous ailments. All mother cats teach their kittens to nap daily.

Naps can be five minutes, fifteen minutes, thirty minutes… but not much longer. The secret of a nap is to pounce quickly, in and out of it… like a wink. It delights and makes one smile inwardly. Ever hear of a Cheshire smile… Or Mona Lisa?

It is an inward and mysterious smile… like a secret lightning bolt of peace. Blast away… enjoy, and savor the experience.

Like cream. Wow… Cream is a beautiful word. The sound of the Rs are even sweet to speak. The way they roll off your tongue… rrrrr. Saying cream is a reason some cats talk so much. That sweet thick delight, that drives the senses wild. Indulge in it at every opportunity… whipped or straight up, sweet cream is divine.

What we are trying to share with you folks… is relax and enjoy life more. Enjoy the pleasures of life. Don't be afraid to indulge yourself when you can. It gives balance to the hard times, that come to every life. Nobody can escape the challenges of health and loss.... but having a little cream time, somehow balances it all.

It is beautiful to be alive, to grow and explore, love and grow, laugh and sink, drink cream and eat fish, get massages and sunbathe and moon bathe... Garden with the worms... and harvest dreams... Open up your life to the essence of cream in every one of your nine lives... Maybe more...

There once was a cat
Named Mona Lisa
She was a Persian ancestor
Of many champion Scottish Folds
Who lived and dined on perfect pillows
Of red silk

She being the cat of an artist
as well respected, as a muse
She grew a luxurious blue- black coat
Very long
That gleamed with a glow

Her smile held mysteries
And her person used to bask
In the light
Of her eyes
That held a sage like glow
Hypnotizing him
To paint

There is a famous portrait
Of such a woman
Who has remained an unknown mystery
Through time
And all educated cats know
That Mona Lisa's smile
Was transformed
And captured there forever

She was a Queen to him
And was fed
Her cream, whipped up
After dining, she would purr for him
With delight
It all began in Italy
But a century latter
It would become a fashionable dessert topping
In Paris
Creme fouette

That was brought to Paris
By a Russian Blue
And her person
A young Baroness
With a love of all things sweet
On her Honeymoon

The Creative Chapters

Guide 9

The creative benefits of whole cream and joy.

Don't do anything halfway, or almost. Don't... Just do love, and be...

Climb high... and enjoy the view!

Clean your ears, or anything else you want do of importance (and everything you do is important)... with full purpose, forging forward. You cannot imagine how that will change things for you. You cannot imagine how dull thinking half and half (as we call it) is to us cats. We like cream, pure and simple, delicious... divine cream. On the rocks, warmed, steamed, iced, with a touch of the sweet, will give you energy to live your life. If you enjoy whatever you do with a full heart and appetite for life.

At least we find that to be so...

We cats hate diets, starvation, and low fat foods. We find that by living joyfully we do not need to take the halfway paths most people seem to fall into. Halfway here, halfway there... not really going, or being anywhere special.

Paint the windowsills of your house purple and orange… and open up your windows. The wind flows inside, like the sweet smell of jasmine on the wisp of a balmy wind opening up your windows to let the air within, and the dust fly out. It will allow you to become more a part of life, and once you connect to life, everything changes and shifts. It's the place of creative inspiration. It is the halfway measure of life, in the holding back, that life creates boredom and fear. Fear is the enemy of creativity. It kills joy at the root.

Joy is contagious, and can be swallowed whole. It is vital and it burns more calories than exercise. When you are bored with your life, or have no joy… you will munch treats and calories double and triple time without thinking. Some trans are fine, as a snack… but don't eat them out of boredom. Climb a tree instead. If you eat whole foods, and foods part of the vibrancy of life… you will stay in touch with the joy of being alive.

Some cats are in awe of the raw foods, sushi lover, and tuna. They inspire their people to buy blenders to juice and enjoy the fine fruits and vegetables, that are good for people. Other cats prefer rich gravy proteins, and inspire their people to cook the gourmet food in life, long lists of ingredients, elaborate cream sauces.

Whatever way you go it is important to lap up the joy. There are numerous ways for people to prefer food. We cats enjoy the diversity in the many styles… as much as people.

Our advice with food is to hunt for the finest food that excites you, and pounce and prepare. Never eat out of boredom. It is too stale. We love to grab throughout the day, and find it gives us energy to find the perfect perch to nap on… or whatever it is. You want to do. We love love love protein…

Gemini thinks that cat people may need more protein than non-cat people. But she is not totally sure of that one, so I will write it with a question mark of 2? She says that one thing she knows for sure is that there is lot of lack in the nutritional value of most people's food. We cats have heard there is a slow foods movement for people, and love the concept. People do too much, too fast… and fast food is an example of how poor nourishment fastness can be.

The one ingredient that we know that is helpful to all beings is happiness. The path to happiness in simple. You may need to learn it form your cats. It oozes in the purrs. Cuddle and pet, play and nap… let your cat guide you gently into joy.

Look deeply at life, let the eyes of your cat light you up. Connecting with others deeply, without an agenda is another freebie that nourishes and heals. It's also very fun to do. Gazing into crystal balls is a good way to practice. We think any time you really see someone more deeply, it is grounding to the body and soul. People can be so superficial. If you fall deeply into the mystery of life, that will take you to places… you can never imagine… just being with someone, and deeply sharing their presence… can be so uplifting… and there it is. Another freebie.

When you look into your cat's eyes with love, it flows from you to them like a thick web of honey. You connect deeply and completely. A few slow blinks enhances the tie. We know it is not easy for people to do anything really important… so we will teach you. You should probably practice connecting deeply with your cat, before trying it with another person. And when you are ready to try… be certain you try, with another cat person.

Every cat is a little different, in what makes them comfortable in life. People are the same that way. It takes patience and effort if you want to have a buddy. Sometimes it takes lots of patience, like when there is a misunderstanding or a hurt heart. The reason isn't really as important, as the healing. Sometimes just saying you are sorry and being quiet for a period of time holding love in your heart is all it takes. Love is patient and kind. There is nothing in the universe more beautiful than healing and licking a friend you can trust.

People are more complicated as they cannot seem to sit still long enough to unravel their thoughts and really tune in. Often they have to go to a bar or ingest a drug to just sit comfortably and quiet and listen. The next day they often forget what they heard. It's unbelievably easy for them to complicate the simplest problem that way. We say the words simple and complicated a lot, for obvious reasons. Once again you can turn to your cat for assistance. Gemini wonders how people who have no cats, survive at all. She said having a cat may be your only hope. (Sometimes tortoiseshells get a little intense.)

When you bond with your cat, or cats, it does help if you have three or four… it can really do wonders. It can be really exhausting work, helping a person. Many of them have no clue how to understand anything. They cannot help it. They are just lower on in the evolutionary scale or something. We really love our people, Gemini says, so we try and try to help… but it sure helps to have other cats to share in the responsibilities.

Bonding is a lot about joy… When you feel good within yourself… it is easier to admire another. Try noticing something special about your cat each day… a pink paw, a folded ear, an adorable nose… Just thinking such thoughts will light you up. Then turn to yourself… find something really special, and feel good about it… Think about that special unique quality for a day or two, here and there. It will put a smile on your face and light you up. Then start thinking about a special quality you admire in another cat friend… or human. If you are brave… share your feeling, and watch the joy light up. There is a lot more to this, we are keeping it simple, starting at the beginning. However even these small steps are incredibly powerful. Such steps taken seriously will generate huge shifts.

Or you can go to a bar and order a shot of cream. Straight up!

May you leap
Like a frog
On a quest toy
In a circle
Going sideways
And unsaid down
To new destinies
Of mystery
Finding secret
Strengths and keys
Of wonder
As you lap
A bowl of cream

While every heartbeat
Leads you forward
With new cycles
Letting go clumsily
Of old skins
Growing greener as you
Grow
And unload
In the ripples
Of the deep blue
Still and true waters
Of trust
As you lap
A bowl of cream
And a sardine

As you engage the lovers of life
May you find joy
And kisses on the wind
While hugging trees
As the deepest waters
Caress your soul
With new beginnings
Surrounding
All fear
To the larger discoveries
As you lap
A bowl of cream

Guide 10

Creating Luck

Gemini thinks it wise to discuss the subject of luck with you. To be truthful she got a few of the cats to look up at that one. It seems to be a subset that is elusive to cats and people alike

> Luck is a feather
> The fashion statement of an angel
> Very light to carry
> But can and will fly away
> With any passing wind of doubt
>
> It is wise to hold onto
> And at its best
> It is carried, on a purple hat
> Or a light heart
> Who expect the world
> To be a place of magic
> Adventures
> And true love

Some call luck a fool
But every cat
Will tell you
It's a large part of the success
Of every great hunter
And some of the young cross their paw
With superstitious hisses on full moons
The ancients know
Its mystery is expectations
And its source
Is soul deep
A gift from a past life
Returned
Or created to carry on
Like wings

You may want to think about that poem for a while. Gemini often says that attitude and expectations are the key… What you expect in life, you receive… Yet there are deeper mysteries, that impact our paths, unseen and shimmering with power…

Several of the old cats rolled over, and whispered a few unkind things about Gemini when she received this poem. Crystal had to put out a number of plates of salmon with sauce to quiet the room. Dave was still asleep, so the talking was quiet, along with the usual telepathy carried out in the presence of most people.

Crystal just kept passing out the food plates, and listened. Several of the oldest grumpy cats gave her pumps on the head of approval for the feast. And then fell asleep...

But the young, and the young of heart... listened deeply and digested her words, after a few choice treats.

Then Crystal, usually quiet... with a nod from Gemini shared a secret tale. Once when she was young, eight or nine, Crystal told a man of importance she would never marry unless it was to a prince or a cat breeder... "Creating her path of destiny and luck." Gemini interrupted... the discussion went on a while... The young kittens discussed the matter of luck for hours, while they batted a ping pong ball. It is good to be young, and open to new philosophy.

By then the older cats were snoring... Even Crystal and Gemini cuddled up close.

All of a sudden Qwilleran walked into the room, or rather swaggered... He had been listening to the whole conversation, and decided he should give a little speech.

Just to clarify a few things... When Qwilleran spoke to the cattery, everyone listened. He cleared his throat, and began...

"Let me just say that Gemini is a most amazing cat... But she sometimes does get carried away. When I was a kitten..." he began. Now several of the kittens thought Will was just born a cat... and never even was a kitten. Apparently a myth. Will had long black fur, that gleamed. His ears were tight, and his eyes were the eyes of an old soul. Gleaming amber guides. He was the cat who brought

Mom to Montessori Cattery, and he was her number one. Some say she loved him best, right after Dave. Others said Dave was second to Will. Either way, he was important. The youngest kittens through he was an emperor. He did nothing to discourage the myth.

"When I was a kitten," he continued… "I knew I had an important mission in life. I walked right out of the room now called 'Ron's Folly' into the living room, with a high tail. Dave and Caprice laughed at my self-assurance at six weeks. Then Crystal living in NJ had a dream about getting a long haired Scottish fold black boy, with folded ears to take to a cat show. Show up, I did…" he said proudly. "I made Grand Champion before I was two… and the rest is history. And that," he added, "was in the old days… when you had to do more than show up, at a show… to get the ribbons!"

Everyone was quiet, thinking… including Qwilleran… Thinking what had happened next in the history of the cattery. How Caprice had died of an infection, and David was broken hearted… How Crystal had visited, and how David and Crystal had become great friends. "They only fell in love because of me," Qwill continued… "and that is not a matter of luck. Or perhaps I was the great luck charm," he thought, chuckling to himself.

All the kittens were quiet, they could not imagine the cattery without Mom here. They were sure glad Qwill or luck had brought her home.

"It may be after all that such luck comes from the fights of a past life." Gemini began to speak to the room, in the silence of Qwill. Some of the cats remembered their past lives, and agreed with that possibility.

"How do we cultivate such good luck from the best?" they asked Gemini eagerly, as past lives were diverse.

"I am go glad you asked," she said with her tail straight up with a questioning curve at the tip. "It is so simple... Be grateful, and expect it. In so doing you also create it, for the future and your future lives..." You could hear a toy bow drop on the floor, the room was so quiet as they all contemplated her words.

Qwill stood up, and said simply... "It is a little more complicated than that, but it's a good place to start." And although they all expected him to continue talking, he said no more. Dave was awake, coming down the stairs. He was tripped by two young teenage kittens... Pepper and Angus... who were playing with Dave's robe. Dave was not amused.

"Some kittens know how to make bad luck for themselves," Gemini continued, and everyone laughed quietly to themselves... as Dave fell into his favorite chair. Crystal ran to make some coffee, and the cats scattered about. Several jumped in Dave's lap to cheer him up. It was not working so well... The discussion dropped for the day, but the subject is frequently discussed. Gemini suggests you read the next poem several times to yourself.

She wrote it the night she wooed Fluffernutter. Ooh la la!

It was a full moon night she remembered with a Cheshire smile.

Create your lucky
Star
Believing in
The shining
In the dark and listening
To the lost lore of the full moon stories
And their secret portents

Hiss away at impossible dreams
And pounce forward
With your tail high
And curled over the tip
Today you are in heat!

Making discreetly
A new trend
In what is fashionable
In the spotlight creating your destiny
Of ribbons and
True love
With the red cat
In the corner of your dreams.

Creating luck is like creating life. Believe in luck and good fortune as the wheel of life turns on. Gamble a little to practice. We cats love to jump from high places to explore luck. People can play poker or wear a lucky charm.

You have to stretch and smile to be lucky. Throw caution to the wind, and sail through the wind, in a boat, on life itself. To believe in life and happiness is to create luck… My sister Lynne used to crochet tiny sweaters for newborn babies with different patterns and colors so they could grow up free thinking.

When you create luck, you create opportunity. When you open your mind, heart and paws… life opens up to you. It's simple, and dazzling like chimes ringing on the wind. The world is yours, be free and play. May your play be full of pounces, and naps, stretches and cream, visions and dreams created. But most of all, may your life be overflowing with bonds of love and sharing purrs.

Stay close to your tortoiseshell cats. They will lead you in the right directions if you get lost along the way. There are several chapters on creativity and cream. They are important points on the game of life to stay close to if you get stuck on a challenging day. That is how the whipping of cream, and good luck desserts were invented… in the last century. You can read about it in *The book of Cream and Gravy Recipes*.

Guide 11

On Creating Opportunity

Gemini is washing her two tone face that reminds Crystal of Carmel and Cocoa to a very clean place, as she considers the topic of opportunity. It is one cats never have to think about. They just pounce on opportunity, when they see it. Copy us!

Crystal waited a long while, before realizing that was all Gemini had to say on the subject. There was a long awkward silence, in the room. Crystal cleared her throat several times, even hummed a tune… before Gemini looked up with mischief in her eyes.

"I see." She purred softly. "You do not have a clue," Gemini said in a gentle voice. Crystal began to make a flower arrangement out of roses to avoid the awkward silence, hoping Gemini would continue… Thankfully the roses seem to inspire her. Gemini always loved roses, and thought they tasted delicious. The lavender and peach roses were her favorites. For those of you, who still have the delusion that cats cannot see colors, please be advised that cats prefer gold to silver, with copper being a close third.

And so Gemini began again. "This is an easy one. It begins with being attentive to the small details of life. Keep reminding yourself to pay attention all the time… as you never know when a mouse or an opportunity might come around the corner. If you remind yourself to stay aware… it will become a lovely habit. Good habits, like attentiveness, are very good to cultivate. Looking about frequently is a fine place to begin. It is only the beginning consciousness, but you do have to see what is around you. After you become accustomed to paying attention, you have to practice sitting… looking, and seeing, with focus. Notice the flowers budding on the orchid, and tune in closer. I, call it zoning in.

"You have to learn to see the details," Gemini continued… "The dry soil the needs water. A small bug underneath a leaf, beginning to make trouble. Weeds. People ignore weeds, and that is what gets them into trouble. See the details…"

She continued with greater animation… and Crystal kept creating the rose arrangement.

"The universe likes to throw out opportunities every day, all around us. A can of half-eaten tuna, in the garbage… a sandwich… such treasures can create a wondrous afternoon. Once you begin to look and see, you will find them everywhere. Jobs on the internet, love in your backyard, creativity in a ball of yarn. It's all there, once you allow yourself to slow down, and notice the synchronicity. Synchronicity is meaningful coincidence. Cats live by synchronicity and intuition. People need help, believing in such powers… but they are real, and they are there for all who wish to enjoy them. Why make life so hard, as many people do… when they do not have to. The people who learn to embrace them, are the ones you admire…

"If you need something, ask the universe… and pay attention to messages and synchronicities that are sure to follow. Begin to look about, and see… and enlarge your expectations… and you may be surprised at what comes your way, even while napping. The horizon is wide…

"When you are ready… pounce, parachute jump, make a shuffle or fall in love… "

Get ready for the adventures
Of life
Every day, is a new beginning
A creative force
Of synchronicity
And a pounce

How far can you jump?
Do you even know, without trying…
You can only leap on Pillow Mountain
So long, kittens…
And then you must move on…
Where your spirit takes you

And leap
With the good faith
Of a cat
Knowing that failure
Is the stepping stone
To success
In the great hunt

And the thrill
Of the journey
The south wind
And the winding river
Have the most beautiful
Rainbow fish shimmering with color
And delicious success
Carpe Diem

After a little catnip, Gemini once told Crystal that she learned about opportunity as an alley cat in Rome from her mother Celeste, many, many, moons ago in another life.

She still retains a love of everything Italian from opera to spaghetti.

Guide 12

On youth and Kittenhood

It's cute to have a smudge on your face as a kitten. As an adult, wash it off or get a facial. Use a sandpaper cream to clean well and glow. It' s adorable as a kitten to have a fluffy loose knot. As an adult it can lead to some extreme issues, like being taken to a groomer for a Lioncut. Groomers should be avoided. Often they smell like dogs that are not taken care of. They bathe with tidal waves... Luckily with our nine lives, we usually survive. It is far better to avoid the groomers altogether, by aging gracefully.

Crystal gave up climbing trees on her birthday. We all respected her decision.

Now she is learning to make Bonsai trees. Everyone is wondering if she is going to try to climb them...

Crystal has also read about a cat groomers association that is different. She wants to take Earl Grey to South Carolina for three weeks to study at their school. Dave is not so excited about it. Earl Grey is even less enthusiastic. Ear Grey is a long haired Scottish fold kitten, with a tendency to trap poop under his tail. It is not glamorous or elegant to hold on to poop. Let the small shit go, as they say...

If you want to know more about it, look for the coming book, *Spa Treatments and Tsunami Tidal Waves*, this spring.

The message from the cats is... don't act like a kitten when you are a cat. Age with grace, agility and dignity. Keep your head high on your shoulders and blink slowly. You may not have everyone laughing to tears with flip antics, but is that what you really want. It's one thing to laugh with a kitten, and another to be laughed at as a cat. Being elegant is about knowing how to be cool. Stache, Qwill's mom could jump at 10 years, higher than most of the kittens. Very high... over a bead, and land as delicately... as though she were flying. She really knew how to be a cool cat. She loved French food, and Brie cheese was her favorite!

Just absorb this message, and take a nap.

I met an old cat
On a couch pillow
One afternoon
Basking in the sunshine, that glowed around him
In ripples
He was a wise one
And everyone loved to listen
When he spoke
Which was not often

I asked him once
His opinion on kittens
He coughed up a hair ball
Before replying
"Kittens are Barbarians,"
He said, rather loudly
"But they are so cute… you must admit,"
I replied, a bit disappointed

"Yes, they are."
He gave me a small smile
"From a distant perspective," he continued
"But never up close
And personal."
And that is all that he would say. I tried to further engage him
In talks of past and future lives
And he just changed his position
With a yawn

After a long nap
As the sun was setting
And he was having an early dinner of sardines
He was more open to my discussion

"The thing is," he said, "cats try to be like kittens
And make endless fools of themselves
Trying to be who they are not
Be who you are, I say.

"A cat is not a kitten. We are civilised
A part of the world society
Where I learned to appreciate sauce
And serenity
And good conversation
Such as these.
I have heard," he continued,
"A cat was involved in the invention
Of bit coins and cyber finances

"Kittens talk about jumping pillows
And have the shortest whiskers
What do they know about anything…"
He replied grumpily
"They cuddle very well," a nearby mother cat put in
And everyone looked at her
Nobody challenged the grumpy old cat, nobody
Who could barely remember his kitten days.

But she was a new mother
Marsh-mellow
And she loved her kittens with a great passion
And would not let him speak
Without interjecting
Her whiskers were long
And her long white fur shimmered
As she spoke up, with eyes round and beautiful

The debate went on late
Into the evening
And the old grumpy cat
Seemed to like having the attention of beautiful Marsh-mellow.
If only for a philosophical difference
Of opinion

In the end Marsh-mellow
Got so upset she hissed
And the old cat swiped at her
But regretted it instantly as she retreated
To attend her kittens,
And moved them

One small gentle tabby teen
Named Stripe
Stepped over to the old cat
And curled up around his tale

The old cat, started to object
But stopped himself
Suddenly remembering
Climbing a cabinet of fine china
And being forgiven after the great crash

Gemini stepped in then
Quickly… gently moving
Stripe along
It is good
To appreciate
Every phase of life
But being a mother more than once
She was inclined to agree about kittens
Being barbarians
Even as she purred them to sleep
Lapping cottage cheese
And sweet cream

Guide 13

On Maturity and Wisdom

This chapter is about aging with grace, and letting go.

It is often difficult, and requires several lifetimes to do it well, so be patient... and have no expectations.

If you appreciate life, and live every day to the fullest... You will have few regrets when you are curled up on the couch pillows. To live without regrets in an overflowing fountain... that flows into pools of serenity and grace. It helps one to understand the great garden of life, that is a precious gift for both people and cats. That is why Gemini wrote this guide, to help people appreciate life more. Sometimes life is very hard. For cats, too Even if they understand how to live better than people. Circumstances can be daunting. Without cats, many people would be completely lost souls.

Cats are gifted in transformation... but they too, enjoy the sacred relationship of feline and humans that began even before the temples to cats were built in ancient Egypt. It is always hard to let go of on an old friend... but this is part of life. Cats teach humans about dying, by example. They move on more easily, over the rainbow bridge... into the next mystery… Beanie Baby is starting a book on cats and hospice in his mature days.

Crystal and Dave often say… they never live long enough, ever… and you can never replace the ones you loved and lost, but you can fall in love again. We cats suggest, you always keep a cat or two by your side in this life. Gemini suggests you make one of them a tortoiseshell.

As we cats know, and see…beyond death's mystery… all the cats you love are closer than you think. Guiding and loving you… like angels, winking.

There are no ends
Only new beginnings
Although the rainbow bridge
Is a slippery realm
A mystery of loss
And love
Connecting both sides
Evenly flowing and free

Tears sometimes blind
Our hearts with sorrow
But the wise old cat
Who is a bit grumpy
Peeks into the secrets of life daily
In his naps
And smiles
The Cheshire smile

Life is more
Than purrs and fur
It has spirit
And an ageless heart
And life laughs at itself

Guide 14

When you Get Stuck…

If you get really stuck understanding, take a break… Don't try to absorb everything all at once. You might want to go to Jamaica, or better yet Cat Island in the Caribbean. It's not really necessary but changes of environment seem to help people. We cats just change positions. Try both! You may be surprised, where this practice leads you, to discover…

When you change positions, all perspectives change in a flash. We see the world more like a diamond cut into many dimensions of sparkle and fire. We are farsighted and some of us can see into the next dimension—into worlds of ghosts and spirits. Some of us can see far into the future, or into alternative realities as we call them. There are also many alien worlds to ponder. Many of them very wise. Many of you are farsighted, too. You may discover many dimensions both within and without of yourself through these guides.

Remember to not worry about doing anything, just allow these words to flow into your mind, and your subconscious… and into your dreams. The main thought here is we can change our perspectives in a blink by a blink. That is what being a cat gives us. This is a good time to review the blink meditation.

Part 2
Going Deeper

Guide 1

On Moonlight and Nightlife

Moonlight is magic. It gives life the glow... that you see first in our eyes, and then it travels to the skin and fur... and submerges within... only to expand out, into the aura for all the cats and clairvoyant people among you to see. We cats adore moonlight, especially at midnight... We advise people to try to stop sleeping through it, all the time. It is a terrible waste of magical potential. Midnight itself... is, next to twilight of course, the very best hour in the twenty-four to be uplifted by the energies. Many cats revive their energies in the moonlight. It is a fine therapy for depression, grief and the maladies of this life that cannot always be avoided. They all too often bring the spirit down. We suggest you bathe in moonlight at midnight as much and as often as you feel inspired to do.

We know you like to sleep, as do we. There is, we feel, a time and place for all things in life. Sometimes just making a few adjustments, makes all the difference in a life. Moonlight enhances beauty and glamour. It is the best thing to develop sophistication and charm in. It is equally fine clear, with stars… or smoky with clouds. Just sit in the moonlight if you need to get clarity on an issue. It is a lovely time to read Tarot cards (a fine pastime cats have been involved in inspiring since the ancient Egyptian times).

Moonlight is an excellent hair color for older women. It is mysterious, ageless and exotic. Cats call it the blue shades. The young may find it to be a fine streak to play around with. If you are uncertain, and want to experiment, just ask your cat for advice. Preferably a blue solid or blue tabby. Men are also invited to experiment.

Moonlight is the veil of nightlife… a time to be unpractical, make love, fall in love, advance, run, flow, with the creative in life. It is a time to play! It is a time to follow magic and inspire art. It is a time for Turkish coffee and baklava, mint tea and sugar plum, or catnip… as is your pleasure. It is for dreaming and transcending and liberating. Black nights are beautiful and daring. If you feel shy, go get a manicure of icy silver, the color of starlight… and walk around with it. You will become inspired. Many kittens are born after midnight. It is a safe time for transformations…

Do not forget to sparkle like the stars. Wear diamonds, or green demantoid garnets… or any such stone, or sequined fabrics that can sparkle your special qualities in the moonlight.

Every sparkle, however small, is important. You are very special. Each one of you. It is the hope of this guide to help you rekindle that special magic inside of you. Cats know they are unique and sacred. People often get lost and abandon the fullness of their life force to shadows. They live like ghosts of their real selves. Ghosts are perhaps a poor choice of words, as we cats know many merry ghosts who know how to party past midnight... (but we think you understand our drift).

To begin to get back in touch, try to lie in the moonlight an hour a week. You can pretend you are going out to throw out the garbage at first, and then take a seat. Step outside of yourself, and breathe the life of the night. Now some folks get carried away and lie out in the backyard on an electric heating blanket under the full moon, to energize. We cats applaud such boldness. If you are one of these rare people, you probably don't need this guide at all. If you are just starting out on moonlight, keep reading.

Many young people sense their life force is slipping away in the late twenties. They run to the night bars to party, as they say.

We want you to understand you can get lost there as much as any human space. We are talking to you about activating vibrancy, not necessarily a bumbling bar scene. That is not to say that a human night out on the town may not have its charms for you. We just want to be clear... to do what we are trying to do for you has to be done outside in the moonlight. The elixir is energy, not wine. Of all the human endeavors, mountain climbers seem closer to chasing our guide for you. You do not have to climb a mountain, although climbing of any kind is very nice... but it is the energy of the awoken chase of life… that is what we are guiding you to towards.

Enjoy a drink of fire, a smoke on ice… but remember to return to the wild and natural nightlife to be free, and become ageless. Gemini reminds you if you go out at night, to party… to dress in camouflage or tortoiseshell patterns or lace or patent leather. She likes to drink Kahlua and cream, straight up… hold the Kailua. Be careful if you wander a lot in human bars and nightclubs. There are a lot of wolves off leash. Ladies, better to travel in a pack… and keep your claws sharp. Gentlemen, keep your back close to the door… in case you need to leave suddenly and climb a tree. You never know, and it is good to be prepared.

Once you let go of all your expectations, and flow with the energy of moonlight… You will begin to find the key to yourself. It is a small step, but full of vital currents. The life force is alive, and well. It requires no money to engage it fully. There are many curious misunderstandings with money. It does buy sardines… but not life. Just tune in and go with the flow. You will be amazed with the power of the great universal flow. It is strong. Cats lap it up, and thrive… while we watch our pet people blur. Gemini can think of no better word for it. She's busy now, preparing for new kittens that will, she feels, be born on the very next full moon.

Moonbeams
Travel through the spine
Like a lover's caress
Or the pet of a cat
By his favorite mistress

Awakening life
Awakening the current
Of electricity
That soars
And turns us all on
To sparkle
As a star

Moonlight dances
In the dusty clouds, with a subtle glow
And in the clear eyes
That stare into your soul
Bright as stars

Moonlight
Knows the mysteries of life
And wants to share it's secrets
With those who listen well
There is much to hear

Guide 2

On Sunshine and Naps

Sunshine is a big one. We cats all watch and wait to bathe in the sunshine. We do not burn, we gather in the light and energize our beings. Crystal says that Caprice sends us bubbles of joy on sunbeams and moonlight. Sometimes Crystal waves at the stars. We humor her as no cat we know ever seems to get anything out of starlight… but we tortoiseshells like to keep an open mind.

To begin, cultivate a love of light…

A word about people and suntan lotions. Unless you are wearing a fur coat, do the human thing. Do remember that moonlight has no such restrictions for you. Just allowing celestial lights of any kind to flow around your aura and your body will cultivate the glow of light magic. Yes, we cats also do cat magic… but that is in a later chapter.

A word about rain and storms… avoid them. Run, hide and have a few favorite hideouts that nobody knows about… a closet, under a bed, a café, a park, a plane to escape the storms of life. Have two or three in case one door is unexpectedly closed.

You cannot avoid all unpleasantries in life, but you can expect there will be a balance of them you can avoid. Like the vacuum cleaner or a rainstorm, on a Sunday afternoon... when you had the best nap planned. Not everything has to be faced bravely.

And when great tragedy strikes, like a hurricane... or your person dies... Remember Bastet. Bastet, the Egyptian goddess of cats... To petition, for a cat miracle. She is a good listener and most sympathetic. Keep it in your back pocket... And save it. Let us return now, to the sunshine.

Sunshine is a sweet space to rest, a great time to be enveloped in a nap, and it is a wonderful place to breathe in some much needed peace in a busy day. It is no ordinary thing to bask in the rays of the great healer, sunshine. Old bones are warmed back to healthy by its rays... and it slows down kittens into a deep restorative growth spurt.

It is orange juice to the soul. Nothing better for people than eating fresh slices of citrus in the sunlight. Cucumber and celery are also a great refreshing tonic... or it can be café au lait, as is your personal pleasure. We are hoping that you are beginning to understand that although we have some guides and suggestions, we are not constructing your choices. There are many paths, and they change over time. We just want you to stop judging, and becoming rigid. Stretch in the sunlight. Stay hydrated, and the rest... the more whimsical... and musical can begin to take over your spirit. Let the inspiration flourish from within.

Sunlight is a great time to be enriched by great literature such as this guide. Read in the light, as they say, followed by a restorative nap or yoga. It is restorative, the ultimate simple. Sometimes sunshine is a fine prelude to bathe in following an exotic spa treatment. If you follow such a treatment in the early morning sun, or late afternoon on a lounge chair… the benefits will amaze you. We are here to tell you to enjoy all that you feel drawn to explore in life, but the sunshine alone can do it all. That is the simple truth of restoration. Sunshine, and water cures… meditate on that.

Naps, short or long, are always a fine thing any time, anywhere, whenever you can. Just do it! It is especially healing to curl up with a purring cat, if you are fortunate enough to have such good company. You can never have too many naps or too much love. It is a basic essential for strengthening the life forces. Once you connect with the life force, you can create anything. Be thoughtful there… It's a powerful statement.

For now, just read and indulge… in the liquid honey of sunshine, and expect you will be healthy and hardy, and wealthy beyond measure in all that is good in this life. That is a great starting place.

Illusions will remain but you can learn to see through them. We want to talk to you about money a little now. We know it is often a great concern. People see it as an oasis in the desert, and they like to count it. We think they count on it too much. In the end the oasis is often a mirage, and the desert is alive with life… if you know how to see clearly. It is important that you see that just because an illusion may seem real, it may not be. Just understanding that will begin to shift you into a new realm.

We knew a dog once who bit and shredded all his person's bills. The dog tried so hard to help his person, become free... This guide is trying to guide you, and we believe we will have much greater success than our dog friend (however well-meaning he was).

Any time you spend with nature, and natural surroundings like moving water, can enhance emotional and spiritual health in people. We cats like to drink from moving water as we feel it is life giving. We are creatures of the desert, but we know how to find the water. We suggest you get a fountain for your home, and your health... and your cat's pleasure, and amusement. Satisfy all the mysterious thirsts in your life. It will create a profound shift.

Humans live like earthquakes
That are a small part of life
They open up the earth to a fast shifting change such
flowing lava cannot be ignored
And at such times we must go
With the flow of life… and leap

Such days are rare
And until such times
We say nap and be still in the sunshine
And drink in the sweetness
Of the lazy day
With a trembling stretch
And some warm tuna

Profound mystery
Is everywhere
And the answer to every question
Is in plain (and the natural) sight
Of the visionary
Cat napper
With a little catnap

So do try not to worry so
Or count your coins with rapture
Have a little sweet cream
And get lost,
With your cat, in a dream

Guide 3

On Living Fully the Nine Lives

Live the nine lives, and follow your heart fully, wherever your heart leads you to… If you only read this sentence once a day, and live it out fully… this guide will be your great success. There are many other hidden opportunities throughout the guides, if you miss this one.

We advise you to have at least three tortoiseshell cats by your side, to inspire you. Gemini says her newest kittens will be available for your service and to be worshipped in ten weeks. They will inspire you with a balance of individuality and camaraderie… free thinking, and respect for life, with a dash of daring and adventure. What more could anyone need to begin to live the quest that is life with more Tortitude.

Gemini is writing another book on the beginning sentence. She feels it is going to be a challenge for people to embrace how easy it is. Her next book will be mostly visions and pictures. These guides and a couple of kits are an excellent start. Gemini has a two color face, that she feels may be a clue to one of the secrets that inspired her wisdoms. She has a great ability to see things in different perspectives. She is fast and sure of herself, and she never looks back with regret. She oozes confidence and grace and has a fine sense of humor. She adores a crashing plate, and takes high leaps at every presented opportunity.

One can never say enough about confidence. If you want to believe in yourself, if you are feeling low in spirit, hang around a tortoiseshell gal. They know how to live life, and are all queens. Some of the magic will run off onto you. Feed them a treat, and it will enhance your connection.

Knowing you have nine chances at life can help to make things different for cats. Crystal has a magnet that says 'what would you do, if you knew you could not fail'… It makes her smile, but we don't like it at all. We do not believe in failure, only experiences that enlighten. Ah, the magic of perspective. It's a cat thing.

Understanding you have none chances makes life more daring for cats, Gemini has a few favorite tips… Don't follow rules, express your true feelings at least to yourself, don't hold grudges or they will capture you, run from trouble fast… it's a slow poke, that often does not catch up, steal food but only if it it's delicious, as crime often pays well. Mostly just laugh with life, and live fully present.

Gemini was the cat of a flapper in her last life, and so it's easier for her to remember life is a dance. Seriously she mentions to Crystal again and again… if you do feel blocked in your life… call Crystal at Montessori Cats and adopt a tortoiseshell kitten, or cat. Your life will never be quite the same. They will camouflage all of your short comings by their special brand of magic.

(The cats remind you that Gemini is a bit flamboyant.) There are many paths, quiet paths of wonder… and wild trumpet paths like Robin Hood. You have to find your own. We cannot do that for you, but we can guide you in the direction of a life that is more alive. Cats are a priceless treasure chest.

Gemini's more complete guide is coming up in 2029 if you wish to explore more deeply. It is mostly visions and pictures, but very transformational. However, she says this is really all you need. Read it again, more slowly… as the messages are there… hidden in between the words when you listen with your soul

'Purr More, Hiss Less' as it says on Crystal's bumper sticker.

There once was a cat
Named Robin Hood
After a wonderful character
His person read about
And so wished he could become

Hal, Robin's person
Read books of adventures every night
And ate lots of chocolate truffles
He worked at a boring computer job
And felt his life to be lonely and hollow

Until one night
He bought the son of Gemini
Into his life
I am not going to tell you
He took up the trumpet
Although he did learn to play a guitar
For Robin was fond
Of music

On a Sunday afternoon
While he was playing guitar in the park
He met
And soon married a lovely lady
Named Mary Ann
With violet eyes
She dances ballet
And encouraged Hal

To quit his job
And make gourmet chocolate
For her pleasure

Hal did quit his job
Although not at first
He waited and worried
And then
On Robin's first birthday
He opened up a new business
From home
Selling truffles online

And became a millionaire
By accident
From a lottery ticket
He purchased to pick up some poop
When Robin missed the litter box
Going home from the vet

He calls the mansion he built
The Cat's Meow
And has taken up painting
Cat portraits
And climbing trees
With Robin

There is just no telling
What a tortoise cat

Or even the son of a tortoise cat
Can do for your life
Mary Ann still loves to dance
And is getting her own kitten
In the spring

Guide 4

On Avoidance and Masks

Since this book was begun avoidance and masks have each become quite a popular topic for people. Social distancing... We cats understand such things well. Trying to keep up immunity during challenging times is actually quite the challenge. Fortunately, we, the cats in your life... can guide you in this endeavor quite satisfactorily. We are actually quite adept at it, having been practicing social distancing when we needed to through time. There is no point in being modest, we excel at it. Even when the times change, and they will...

It is a good skill to be able to manipulate at will...

The key here is to be able to flow in and out of social distancing with charm and grace. It is a multidimensional skill that is very dynamic in nature. It is based on healthy caution, not fear. The last sentence is powerful. And should be read over twice, at least. Fear has its place in a bathtub or a battle, not in everyday life. Even death, the natural leaping point into the abyss that people are often so fearful of... is merely, an unknown, a natural transition never to be feared.

Cats cosily distance much of the time. It gives us perspective within our environment. When one can observe one's surroundings, one can be prepared and steady. This is certainly an area that bipedal folk could use a great deal of improvement in, in our opinion. What we are getting at is that social isolation is an opportunity for people to slow down and start paying more attention to the details.

Yes, it also creates a space for virus and bacteria to be less fertile, and has many medical advantages that I am sure you are quite familiar with. It impacts immunity in more subtle ways that we would like you to explore. When you keep some space around you physically... you can also create a clean aura.

Cleaner auras are the central core for good health and vibrancy. When one keeps a distance, one does not collide and pick up everyone's energy in the room. This energy transfer often confuses the more sensitive folk.

We speak from experience. Cats frequently become ill when their favorite person is unwell or even upset. We are highly sensitive beings and pick up and internalize discordant feelings and thoughts. People do this often as well, especially as we said the sensitive ones... and are often unaware of it. The result is often seen in unexplained moods, poor digestion and a host of other illnesses... both small and large.

We highly suggest people continue to practice social distancing way beyond the time of COVID viruses. The cats have been advising this to Crystal for some time now.

We practice what we preach with great success. If you observe us, most cats have periods of the day of social isolation. The importance of it is central to having inner peace and a good purr. Over our times in social isolation, we cats groom. We tidy ourselves up a bit, quiet our thoughts... and observe our surroundings.

When we leave social isolation to engage with others we know exactly where we stand in a room both physically and energetically. We know the dangers that exist, the windows and doorways we could exit. We know the high perches, and soft pillow places. We also get in touch with the energy of the room. These shifts are often a result of a technique we perform as we groom. It is a little like the human technique of Reiki. It is called Whisperlinking. There is a legend of a cat named Esmeralda who taught her human companion Thea how it is performed in her old age. Qwilleran is writing a book about their lives, scraped up from legends and expanded into historical fiction. It takes place in ancient Egypt in the golden ages, when cats were worshipped as gods and goddesses. It is also quite technical and expands on whisperlinking in great detail if anyone is into a serious study of the practice.

It will be published in 2025 if our plans are on schedule. He is even working on a correspondence course. If you are interested, write to Crystal.

Meanwhile, we will guide you here and now, into a brief exercise to clean our aura of virus and low toned moods.

WHISPERLINKING

STAY SIX FEET OR MORE APART FROM ANY OTHER ANIMALS OR ALIENS
TAKE SEVERAL DEEP BREATHS THAT ARE LONG AND QUIET
  BRING THE BREATH SLOWLY AND DEEPLY INTO YOUR CORE
  HOLD IT THERE WITH THOUGHTS OF LOVE, OF SELF APPRECIATION
  RELEASE IT AND ENCOURAGE ALL THAT IS UNWELL TO FOLLOW THE BREATH OUT OF YOUR BODY
  ACTUALLY INVITE THE ENERGY OUT POLITELY AND ALLOW YOUR AWARENESS TO EXPAND…

  You can continue this technique as long as you need to, and include it with some serious licking or a jacuzzi bath. You can also use a body loofah sponge or a sandpaper tongue to conclude it. It can be done slowly and include a full manicure and pedicure. It can also be done quickly to recharge the senses. Sometimes it can be followed by a bit or protein or vanilla ice cream for a super change. (That is how Qwill does it.)

That is obviously quite a brief understanding of Whisperlinking. Qwill is tilting his head to the side, telling me he has to write his book. Now! He also says to tell you the exercise is a good place to start, and practice for now. Legend says that Esmeralda taught Thea in the twilight hours very quietly, so as not to disturb the other people resting nearby. Legend goes further to say, that the word whisper trickled down into the human vocabulary through a careless conversation. Although Thea was a great magician in her day, she was often impulsive and careless... about many things. It's all in Qwill's book, and quite a story to read, I must say, if you like mystery, adventure and a little romance.

Social distancing can begin and end with a wink. If you stay tuned in... you will move in and out of it, without anyone really being aware of it. Some people say, stay safe. Others say, stay strong... All fine thoughts, we cats prefer to say... Stay alert! Allow awareness to keep you on your paws at all times. We understand social distancing is a space, in a place. It is also much more on the inner realms. It is an inner awareness, to be developed with focus and commitment. Then it is displayed with a most casual air, so it seems a natural movement. Some people like to smoke tobacco or herbs. We cats inhale presence. Try it!

As always, practice makes purrfect. Practice guiding your attention with self-discipline so it becomes a habit. Then you can learn to balance behaviors with disclosures. There is a time for closeness, and cuddles... a complete lack of social distancing... It is a time when it is safe to melt into another's aura. Kittens do it all the time but hardly notice what they are doing. Ah, kittens! They will cuddle up, and bite you on the nose… just for the fun of it.

(If you love kittens, you must read Pussy Willow's book on how to Raise a blue girl and other Charmians. The first chapter is just adorable…)

As I said, kittens melt their auras all the time, but as they mature there is a deepening with the connection. Try cuddling with a kitten, then a cat… Woohoo… In these deeper realms each being heals the other's aura with deep purrs. This leads to cleaning away of much disease, and breaking free of dangerous negativity. We don't have time in this guide to go into the more intimate secrets of the practice. For now, we leave that to Qwilleran in his future books.

Whisperlinking heals.

Social distancing… is like most things in life, both simpler and more complex than it appears at first glance. Understanding how to maneuver with it is an expansive and healing path. We encourage you to explore it frequently. Do try it, with greater awareness today.

Your mind has many avenues we will help you to explore. You really need a cat to free you. In order to explore masks, we must go directly to Gemini, the tortoiseshell cat who started these guides in the beginning. Tortoiseshells often have beautiful masks, with secrets soon to be revealed.

Masks are in fashion now. This began in the medical realm, as a protective shield and has travelled into fashion and personal expression. Many people adore tortoiseshells because of their mystery. Others are quite in awe of the magic in their masks. Gemini's mask is split down the center, half red gold and half a deeper brown. Nobody can contain her mischievous style and spirit. She is posing now for a portrait by a young artist that will one day be a grand masterpiece. It will be close in value to the most famous cat painting, *My Wife's Lovers*.

Cats are born wearing masks and whiskers. It gives them an advantage that people can only imagine. We suggest you pounce into the mask scene that is happening, and take full advantage of the times. Buy several different masks to find your favorite kind. Some cats are just born wearing the perfect one. Soon they will go out of style, and you can practice wearing them when you are alone. The key to a mask is its mystery.

When you wear one, you are instantly transformed into another with hidden secrets and shadows. With all the masks about, nobody really knows who anyone is. Perhaps nobody really knew who anyone ever was. It is a passing, but interesting time. Everyone feels a bit uneasy with all the uncertainty and new mystery about. After the initial disorientation, we start to feel compelled to look in the eyes for more communication clues. Cats have known for centuries how to hypnotize with a blink. If people keep wearing masks and reading each other's eyes, there will be a deepening sensitivity in human consciousness. Who knows where it may lead to… Perhaps to a retune to cat worship.

If you are reading this, in a time beyond masks... know that you can still use masks in visible and invisible forms, using visualization. With practice you too can be like a cat and learn to walk in mystery, with or without a mask. You can with this new magic be protected from many mistaken passages, and many viruses. People hold the mask, and their mystery... with awe. Use masks with purpose. Model your cat as you begin to wear masks. Always use excellent posture, when you put on a mask. Walk with grace and listen for Whisper linkings...

There is a rumor
That the human concept
Of social isolation
Was the inspiration
Of a cat
Whose person belonged
To the highest levels of the government
And must remain hidden
For security reasons

There is a rumor
Among the cat population
That whisper linking
Is again surfacing
From the old days
Of ancient Egypt
When cats were worshipped
As gods

Although we are not
gods
We are far superior than you discern
And do like a little worship
In the evenings
With our dinner

After all
We have saved our people
From hunger, and disease
Reducing the lethal rats
So social isolation
Is just another edge
On the cliff

one of many
Many Messages
We gift to you
Listen well
To our purrs
And to the whisper links emerging
Your cat
Will show you how

Chapter 5

On Travel, Abundance, and Sardines

Sardines are divine... Indulge in delicious food, and music as often as you can. Saxophones, and brunch on Sunday morning leisurely in the garden are an excellent way to begin and end the week. Abandon yourself to the pleasures of life. Remember a kitten lives inside of your heart. It's good to get in touch with your inner kitten, let go and enjoy life at every opportunity.

You can tell a good friend by the food they serve, and the gourmet and organic are high priorities on any cat's list. Crystal has discovered that fresh herring, and the canned variety is a pleasure to cats in many international destinations. When traveling she suggests ordering it for breakfast any time it is on the menu... and wrapping it up in a small plastic container, in case she runs into a cat along the day. The fresher the better... Why in Norway... she discovered a cat named Blu, she still corresponds with.

Chimes are wonderful to keep nearby, wooden... metal, bells and all... call out to live life more gently and closer to the soul. Gemini mentions repeatedly how much cats enjoy their music... and it helps them to relax. Being able to relax is so very important. It opens us up to experience the abundance of pleasures of life… like the scent of a rose on the wind. One need not be rich to open up to the abundant pleasures of life. Just live with an open heart, and flourish. Practice makes perfect.

About work, a common trial for people. Gemini says if you learn to relax more, and worry less… you will be led to new opportunities, and may find yourself enjoying work. Everyone has to hunt, but many rats live on the rivers of life. Life will bite you, tease you, or gift you. It is the way you approach and engage in it, that determines the manner you find abundance. Live in wonder, and an open heart and spirit… and you will be showered by an abundant flow.

Travel outside of your ordinary rut now, and then… is a good way for people to open up to life, and new ways of being. You will return to your old life with a secret smile. Cats can attain these insights when they scratch another side of a chair, but with people everything is a bit more complex. People have a tendency to make simple things difficult. That is why they so desperately need the company of a cat. When traveling, there is nothing better than meeting a foreign cat with a sardine, and finding an exotic soulmate.

Crystal met Blu
By a river
On a cold windy day
In the early morning dawn
When most folks were sleeping

She opened her can
Of sardines
And he admired
Her perfume

Though they spoke different languages
They understood
The language of the soul
And the purrs began to flow
Like a drunken roar

They met frequently
And one morning Blu
Brought Crystal to his home
And new friendships
Among the people flourished
Over wine and cheese
And cats

Blu's people were artists
Who did portraits of cats
And there is one
Of Crystal and Blu,

In a local museum

They still write
Over many years
And fireplaces
Cuddling up with memories
And stories

Guide 6

Massage and petting, versus lust and love

Enjoy massage and pettings, at every opportunity throughout your life. It is a good for the fur, for the soul, healing for the body and bonding for the heart. Always try to stop what you are doing and pet your cat when she requests it. Remember it is equally beneficial to both giver and receiver. It is very nice by candlelight, before or after dinner... or a leisurely nap. It is divine by the fireplace in the winter, or with a balmy wind in the spring.

It is said that petting a cat on a full moon brings good luck in gambling. We suggest you give it a try and see... Life is often complicated, or seems to be so. It is a fine thing to have a little extra luck, to face life with. Luck is a mysterious force, that few understand. It is said to live on the top of trees in abundance. And can be shared when the right link connects. Be open to bringing more of it into your life.

Sometimes life is challenging. Your best friend dies, there is a miscarriage... such things are a part of every life. Sometimes it is our thoughts, and reactions that make life even more challenging. It is where petting and massage come in to assist. They help to carry off the sadness in a gentle flow. Try to remain untangled with sadness and understand it is a part of life... It is why we must appreciate joy. Keep the pets and massages coming.

Some cats like an occasional dose of catnip, which is fine on occasion. Understand that cat nip pettings and massages can get a little wild for people. If you want to explore it, keep a first aid kit around for bites. It will definitely help you to forget your troubles.

When we start to talk about the wild side, Gemini said it is time to talk about lust. When in heat, it cannot be denied. Leap forward and surrender. Bite a neck, and howl. The kittens are cute if they come later... and they only hang around a few months.

For people it is a little more complicated. Everything seems to be. Our advice is do not confuse lust with love. We cats, never do... Although even with us, when the two come together it is a powerful elixir. The subject confuses people so much, Cashmere will be writing about it in a book he is beginning... *Beyond the Stud, there is the lover*. It is his second book full of poetry. It also has a lot of advice about cuddling... and the story of his first love, Dandylion.

1,
Dandylion
Was the finest of reds
A lady
With sharp claws
And soft purrs

She rules my heart
Even as a ghost
When the moon is full
With memories

Her lick
Was rough and sweet
Her eyes
Like amber mysteries
Of light

She captured my heart
And holds it
Forever
In my dreams
My loving lioness

2,
The Pet
Caressing from the crown
To the sacred sacral
Pathways
The energy flows
Like liquid lava
Traveling down
Her spine
Feeling so fine

Her tail twitches
And rises
Like the pleasures of the chase
Simple and complex
The two handed pet
Ripples through her senses

Healing her body
Mind and
Soul
With a kneading motion
Her tail tingles
With delight

As the trembling vibration reaches into her
Claws and toes opening
As the energy sweeps
Through her
Collapsing tension
By the magic
Of the touch

Guide 7

On Independence

Independence is what keep your mystery, and your sanity. Never let go of it. Jump on every table, be free spirited... and don't listen to rules... You can always find a new adventure to pull you through the sad times, if you maintain your independence.

Even a funeral has flowers to smell. Embrace the sweet fragrance of life but do not get overly attached to one rose bush in the garden. Cats can balance remaining detached with being fully present with life. That is what creates our mystery. It is an art.

Here are some ideas to help you... learn several languages, meow!

Play an instrument, learn a new sport, dance... study painting, or cooking or poetry or philosophy. Find your own ideas, things you would like to learn. Don't define your life with boundaries, leap.

Define your life with a larger scope than your personal everyday... For every day is a new beginning, a journey to be hunted, lived, explored. Being present at every moment helps you live with a rare richness. Now and the then... out of the blue, disappear, or yawn with a presence of boredom. Independence is a mask that comes on and off. It's never stuck, but available if you need it.

To keep it simple… keep an awareness of it, in your back pocket like a lucky charm… and swing on the stars, when nobody is expecting it… shine!

> Embodying glamour
> When the stars shine
> On your shadow
> And never get caught
>
> Wear a tabby coat
> Of many stripes
> That can never quite
> Define you
>
> Be a cats's cat
> And know you are
> Descended
> From the Lions
>
> And the royal courts
> Of Egypt
> Where you were once
> Commonly worshipped as divine
> Beings

Live proudly
On your kitty thrones
To be admired
Then disappear
Into the mystery

Guide 8

On Leisure and Soft Etiquette

As cats, we love leisure. We demand it. Lots and lots of it... in our everyday routines. It is where we get centered and create our lives. It gives us a magical edge, a special perspective on life. As human you do not understand leisure, and try to fill it up with activity, that often leaves you tired and restless. You have to learn how to be with leisurely essences. It is more of an attitude, than a holiday. When you understand this shift in thinking, you will be able to embrace and access the leisurely flow of life,

Leisure activities require the art of half sleep. Half sleep can be learned by closing one's eyes so they are half open and half closed... and thinking of something that brings you great joy. You never share this secret joy. It is your secret center of empowerment. Practice this, several times a day for fifteen minutes, and it will become a more natural path for you. If you do not have the time during the week, save it for the weekends. After a while you can lose yourself for long periods of time in these leisurely activities, and actually alter your consciousness. Gemini said you have to trust the guides, and not question the ancient wisdom to develop your inner soul. Because it works...

Some of you have been cats, in other lives... and are now trapped in the body of a person. Qwilleran covers this in his book that will be published. These are rare and special cases, and those souls have deep magical powers that can be developed with extraordinary results. We want you to know that every one of you, has the ability to learn through leisure activities, and improve your life. For those of you who stress over money, it may be a great relief to have that totally out of the picture here. We are talking about change through consciousness, and that is a powerful path. Sharpen your claws, and begin... today.

Another extremely important aspect of leisure is the pillow. Have as many pillows as you can manage in your home. Soft etiquette is the study of pillow power. Although cats love silk pillows, any clean and soft material will do. The purpose of the pillow is not just comfort. It allows us to sink into the depths of the soul. When you sink your soul into a pillow... and learn the art of half sleep... You will transcend many of the concerns that keep you restless, and out of sorts. Then you can begin mind leaping... to parallel universes. Pillows are the launching pad.

We are not saying that this will all come at once so do not become frustrated. Patience and practice with open expectations are the key... And will take you there. We just want to give you a glimpse ahead to see what is possible. We also would like for you to understand some of the advantages that your cat can share with you in this life.

That being said, Gemini asked you to not disturb a sleeping cat, unless absolutely necessary… Now that you understand a little bit more. Please do buy pillows, lots and lots of pillows. Feather pillows are quite nice!

Pillow mountain
Is a legendary path
Into transcendence
Right in front of us

And the pathway
To parallel universes
Where understanding life
Comes in leaps
With a quiet presence

Hidden in the ordinary
There is magnificence
And adventure
If you want to go there
Follow your cats
Leading the way

For her it is an easy leap
She travels every day
After her second breakfast
Before her third bath
To refresh her
Perspectives

Guide 9

The way you face, and hide in life...

To begin with, you have to tell yourself deep in your heart and soul... that you are going to open up to life. Then you can shift from being an observer to a participant. It took Honey-belle a ping pong ball, and lots of cuddles, which she at first thought of as rape, before she began to trust life. We do not mean to encourage rape in humans. Mating is a delicate and complicated matter, the subject of a different book.

Honey-belle was born very timid, and her mother Louise was much the same... but Honey-belle became curious about life... and stepped outside her comfort zone, to face it. It was not always comfortable for her. She discovered when you open your heart to the universe, the universe answers you with possibility. And she pounced on it.

Anything is possible. Anything. Say it again... in a whisper, then out loud. Crystal told Honey-belle this over and over again, while pouring Reiki energy into her... and slowly, she began to trust that there were good forces in the world. At least for that day. Sometimes she forgot the very next day, and they had to start all over… it may be the best thing any of us can do. Human and cat. Embrace fully the blessings of today, with an open heart.

Transformation is the key here, that we wish you to notice… what created it exactly… was Honey-belle's innate willingness to move towards joy, or something larger than her fears. To begin with she was red, an especially helpful gift. A few natural redhead humans such as Dave understand that being red gives you a special advantage in life. That's just a birth blessing reds have, and it should be appreciated.

We all of us have birth blessings, and one step to noticing life is to notice and appreciate them. Notice, and appreciate. Notice and appreciate… Very important stuff… to notice, and appreciate. Honey-belle took her red totally for granted… but the gift was and is there for her waiting, as long as she lived… to tap into.

It was her heart opening to life that healed her wounded spirit in the end. She watched a long while, before she began to participate. That is fine. People also watch life through books and movies along lines. It is only when you move from watching to participating that you can fully live life. It is truly a leap of faith.

There are other times when hiding is essential to master. Climb a tree to avoid a flood. It's simple, common sense… to avoid anything that makes your fur wet. Don't deny it, just avoid it. Climb slightly out of reach until the danger passes. Do what you can to keep dry, and be patient.

Life is always changing… and even a cycle of floods will pass.

Cats know the value of patience. People tend to be disappointed when things don't go as they hoped… even disastrous times pass, becoming new beginnings. When things are really complicated, remember that… and remove yourself and take a nap out of harm's way. It is a good thing to have some hiding spaces available in various locations you frequent so as not to have to find a new one in an emergency. We like to go under the bed, or in a closet… but your big bulky bodies prevent such simple solutions. We suggest some alternatives such as going to a library, a bookstore, a boat, a bar, a bar on a boat, a spa, and on occasion an airport… if things are desperate.

There are other ways to disappear… into a daydream. So much can change in one hour. It's remarkable how a short escape can help… Gemini feels the right brain of people is more cat like and urges people to do some reading on right brain science. She says, keep an open path to your right brain, and travel there frequently.

You might also join a club, a cat club is lovely… but fish clubs, flower clubs, sport clubs, all serve the same purpose. Escape!

We do not suggest escaping from all catastrophes. There are some that have to be dealt with fully and directly… In the present with outstretched claws, or teeth (if you have the misfortune to be declawed). Once the danger has passed, it is important to hide briefly, and assess the damage. Do not, I repeat, do not pee on the carpet and let everyone know you are freaked out. It is never necessary, but if you cannot control it… try to be discreet, and in a corner when nobody is looking. Gemini herself admits to having some trouble with that one. Otherwise, try to just move on into a new day. Act cool, like nothing happened on the outside, even if your heart is thumping away. Repeat the mantra 'Nine lives' several times… until you can gain control. Then take a bath or a long shower. Do not forget to clean your face and whiskers. Check for litter in your toes, the usual things…

The balance between the way you face life and hide from life is what we cats call the mystery of living. It is a delicate balance and will take some practice to achieve.

Pounce on it. Remember we can't all be reds… but we can embrace out gifts… some we were born with, and the others that an open heart brings to us. Life is sweet, sometimes bittersweet… but always sweet. Eat a sardine on a tough day, and catch a nap. Crystal always has a few cans keep on ice. (That is for her, we prefer it warm.)

There is a magic in being present in the joys of life, and in gliding through the sad days. There will always be days that are hard, sometimes years… that is part of life. We have to leap forward, and climb a little higher to a new perch. Try herring for a snack to cheer you up… and believe in the future. If you have lived fully, the memories will get you through the rough times

Now we must explore a little deeper, the subject of escape through magic. Something cats are taught at birth. Listen carefully… Magic is alive, everywhere. It begins with a secret smile. Smiling from deep inside of us is charming at any age, and for anyone. It's the first step into the mysteries. Keep pictures of charm and wonder in your heart... and enter into the eclipses, with brave sparkles... and watch the magic beams of life, like a kaleidoscope.

If you are unsure of how to approach this, it is time to turn to your cat... as a guide. They have been guiding people into the magic realm since the old days in Egypt when cats were worshipped as gods. So go find your cat, before you continue... and if you are patient, the magic will start to appear when you least expect it. Behind an overgrown garden, down an alley, the usual places where magic hides... Just be open, to the possibility.

Next do not be afraid to look into and enter the mysteries when they appear. Their magic beams through ordinary life, leading us to different pathways. Take Qwilleran, for example. He did not like to get his nails cut. At ten weeks old, two vets, a vet tech and a muzzle were unsuccessful. Caprice looked into her crystal ball... into the void, of the unknown path... and said, try cutting one nail, at night when he is asleep. In ten days, Crystal was wearing a gold locket filled with his nail clippings...and was feeling rather brave. She almost bit her boss one day. That is a simple but interesting example.

Practice looking at a problem, with a blank screen... and wait, for a new pathway to appear. You may discover a way to time travel. There is much more of that going on than people realize. Only yesterday, Mona Lisa the kitten said she was in Paris, drinking cream at a bar. She claims she was also hunting in the Pyrenees mountains last week. Who knows?

There is much wonder and magic in the world. It takes only a few steps into belief to open up the hidden doorways. The real trick to these mysteries is knowing that nothing is really as it seems for long. Do not get attached to what is there, or why… Just be present in the sunshine today, or the moonlight tonight. And be present with an open heart to life. There is even a cure for fleas. Life can bring unexpected blessing if your heart is open. Life can be a great flea comb of wonder.

If you can master the balance between being in tune with life actively and hiding out from unnecessary worry you will find escaping trouble and embracing joy to be easier to achieve than you ever imagined.

One day a very young
And pretty woman entered
A bar, during a storm
Everyone watched her
And listened
As she ordered a short of pure cream
Straight up
And drank it
Licking her lips

"What's your name, kitten?"
The bar tender asked with a sneering smile
The bar became quiet, as they listened
"Mona Lisa," she said softly.
And licked her lips.
Throwing her head back, with her long black hair
Falling almost to the floor…
As she laughed
And winked

A sudden roar of thunder
And lightning crashed the electricity
And the bar grew dark
At first people were uneasy
But after a few candles were lit
The intimate setting opened up the room
To whispers and sharing secrets
And an evening that soothed
And settled the folks in the room

Like a cat purring in one's lap

The strange woman
Who'd had a few shots of cream by then
In a beautiful low voice
Told stories of her adventure
In a distant land
That made everyone smile
Although they did not really believe she hunted
In the mountains of France
All alone

But they enjoyed her strangeness
In the dark
And she seemed to send
A quiet joy
Through the crowd
That made them feel well
When the lights came on
Everyone wanted to introduce themselves to Mona
But she was gone
And only a few wet paw prints
Were seen on the bar
In her place

The room was silent
Nobody said a thing about her
Although they looked and looked
About the room

For several nights
The bar tender wiped off the prints with a gat motion
And the mystery
Was not spoken of again
Although everyone seemed
To be a little lit up with a curious joy
And ordered Kahlua and cream
More than usual

The Conclusion
(for Now…)

Tortitude, if you are still struggling to understand it… Do not be concerned. It cannot be captured by the will. It is, how shall I say… an elusive presence, that is all embracing, and a free spirit… like a butterfly. Tortitude is an attitude, a little like a moonbeam. It is impossible to hold onto, but difficult to ignore.

Luckily, you now have a powerful guide n your hands. It may seem like an ordinary book, a mere pamphlet left on a dresser on the side of a bed. But you know better. It shimmers with magic and secret purpose, especially so when the moon is full. Watch it in the twilight. It sometimes seems to glow in the dark. It is magical. This book will change your life. It is not so easy to find a copy, as only a limited number have been printed. Destiny has smiled upon you, and heard your call… It is now up to you, to join the journey of a life with Tortitude.

It is highly suggested by Gemini that you find a tortoiseshell cat, as your guiding friend. Gemini is creating kittens right now, who will help a lucky few… along the path. Do call crystal@montessoricats.com as she can be most helpful in heart and soul match making. Such a relationship can and will transform, everything in your world.

As I said, Tortitude is both elusive and magnetic in its form. You can find many books and Zooms on the proper breeding to create a tortoiseshell cat, but few convey their unique presence, beyond their exotic beauty. What is more extraordinary is many do not notice their magic. Imagine such treasures, so close... In our last few words here... we can only say they are truly beyond words. A tortoiseshell cat has to be experienced to be understood. What a vivid and special experience it will be.

Go for it!

There were legends, that tortoiseshell cats were partners with many of the greatest minds and powers in history... writers, politicians, artists, librarians (cats love books) ... and of course magicians. Their presence is always behind the scenes, and curtains.

Gemini heard tales from her mother's mothers that her great grandmother belonged to a baroness, and was lost on a travel tour of the Americas. She expects a lot from her kittens, but they are extraordinary.

Tortoiseshell cats are almost always females, and make excellent mothers and sages, not necessarily in that order. They combine two colors, other than white. Some of them have colors that blend together, and are more introspective. Others have larger patches of color that are distinct, such as Gemini, whose face is both caramel and chocolate. There are a great variety of colors, from cream to red, and blue to black... but they are all very beautiful.

Exotic, unique in gifts, as well as colors. No two tortoiseshells are exactly alike. They are special cats, with special powers.

If you hold one close to your heart, in body and spirit… you will be lifted to their realm. Be charmed, and live a life of magnificence.

We would like to tell you a bit about the history of Montessori Cats Cattery, where the most magical of Scottish fold cats are raised. If you are lucky, very very lucky… you can adopt one for yourself.

It all began, years ago… when Caprice and David began the cattery. It was well over thirty years ago, although Gemini said that they have been raising cats in past lives in Egypt in the temples. The cattery started as a rescue of sorts. Cats, people, anyone who entered the cattery's touch seem to be rescued.

Over time, Caprice and David wanted to invest all their time into cats. They went to a CFA national cat show, and were enchanted by a long hair, all white, blue eyed Scottish fold female. She began the line as first queen. Caprice could tell you many tales, and perhaps she will channel a book in the thirties called *Caprice's Charms*. Her beauty and charm as you may have heard were legendary. She was also brilliant. She studied genetics, and botany and metaphysics. She taught classes in the evenings on a variety of subjects. Of course, being a Montessori schoolteacher, inspired the name of the cattery.

Without David, the dreams would not have taken root. He is the heart and soul of the cattery. Mothers wait until he is home to give birth, as he rubs their tummy… and cuts just about every cord of the newborn kittens. Including Qwilleran who is sitting by my side. He told me he must be mentioned at least once or twice… until his book is written, *Black Magic and Mystery*.

Qwill, as he likes to be called, was born ten years ago on May 2nd when the sun was in Taurus. He became an important link in the Montessori chain. Crystal was a bit of a quirky woman, who lived her life by the saying 'A woman with a black cat, can do anything'.

Eleven years ago, she had just lost a soulmate, her black cat Julien. She was in deep grief, and went to see an animal grief counsellor… for a little healing comfort. The counsellor asked Crystal if there was anything she had always really wanted to do that she had never done. After some deep thought, Crystal told the counsellor she had always wanted a show cat, and to show a cat in a cat show. "Wonderful," the counsellor said… "Go to a cat show, and get one!"

While Crystal immediately felt better, it was not quite as easy as she thought it would be. She enjoyed many a cat show, with many a cat breed. She read books, talked to folks… but she could never decide on one breed over another. They were all so beautiful. The counsellor could not understand, but encouraged Crystal to keep on looking. And then, one night, Crystal had a dream…

A voice told her to buy a long haired black Scottish fold male cat. Crystal woke up from the dream at three a.m. and looked on the computer. She had never even looked at

Scottish fold kittens. She put the words in the computer 'Black long hair Scottish Fold male kitten'… and there was a picture of baby Qwilleran, ready to take on the world. Crystal could barely wait until morning to call.

Yes, he was available to reserve. The course of true love does not always run smoothly. Crystal asked a friend, who lived in Florida nearby the cattery to visit the cattery, and look Qwilleran over. If you could see the look Qwill is giving Crystal now, you would laugh. Now David and Caprice thought that Crystal's friend was the one who wanted Qwilleran. When Crystal called a few days later, to leave a deposit… they told her, he was adopted already. It was heartbreak all over again. A week later Crystal called Dave and asked to be on the waiting list for a kitten like Qwill. After a bit of excitement, and explanations, and laughter… all the misunderstandings were… well understood. Several weeks later Qwilleran came to live with Crystal.

Crystal became great friends with Caprice. They talked daily. So much so that Caprice encouraged Crystal to move to Florida instead of California. "We need you here," she said simply, over and over again. It was a strong pull… And so Crystal bought a small house in Delray Beach. Delray is a small charming town near the sea, with boutique hotels and little shops. All seemed to be going happily ever after. Crystal put a deposit on two more kittens. Then tragedy stuck.

If a cat purrs
With your sadness

Know that a healer
Walks by your side

And so it was for us, that year. David and Caprice got the flu and were very ill. Crystal called every night. Although she had purchased a house in Florida, she was still living in New Jersey. She had never met David and Caprice in person. Caprice died suddenly, of complications of the flu, and a butterfly left the Earth. We were in deep shock. Dave was devastated... as was Rocket, her special cat who never left her side.

All the cats at Montessori grieved. Crystal moved to Florida with tears in her eyes, The last thing that Caprice had said to her was, "I'm sorry." It was a very very sad time at Montessori Cats, when Crystal first visited to pick up Cashmere and Collette, her two new kittens. They were brother and sister, two little creams puffs.

Cashmere became a great lover, and poet. He is a long haired cream folded ear cat, and his sister Collette is a calico. She is the only Scottish fold who has one straight ear, and one folded ear that we know. She is another legendary beauty, a feminist who refused to have kittens. She wanted a career of her own, and took up modeling, and reading Tarot cards. She occasionally still eats them.

Shortly after Crystal moved to Florida, she went to the cattery to pick up Cashmere and Collette, and met Dave. They became great friends. And later, much to their surprise, they fell in love. We often tell people... you can never replace the ones you lose, but you can fall in love again. We know, because it happened here to us.

Crystal did the best she could to help Dave with the cattery... kissing kittens on the belly, and playing with them. It was hard work, but someone had to do it.

Before she died Caprice told Crystal to please help Dave with the cattery when you move to Florida. Crystal promised she would help, never thinking destiny was calling her. Caprice continues to haunt the cattery lovingly. Rocket went to join her, five years later...

Shortly after David and Crystal were married, Gemini was born. A tiny little girl... with a face of two colours, caramel brown and dark chocolate. She was a little sprite, and carefree. No one would have ever imagined she would become a sage. She could fly over the room, and knock over anything her way... without looking back. She adored David's cat massage and Crystal's music.

Several years later, on New Year's Eve... she gave birth to one kitten. He was a cream colored boy, and she literally sat on him like an egg. He nursed so much, he nursed so much... After a time, even he wobbled off to his own destiny in his forever home. Gemini was inspired by him to philosophize about the meaning of life. One night, after he left home, after Crystal had a few glasses of fine Beaujolais wine... they began the guides together.

And so here you are!

The future of the tortoiseshell cats, knows no bounds. Most people do not get a torty, as they are lovingly called as their first cat. It is usually a second or third cat. They have an exotic look, that David thinks scares some beginning cat people. Crystal thinks that the other cats lead the way to a tortoiseshell. Gemini says to just start out with them, and do not waste time.

The tortoiseshell comes in many breeds, from ally cats to Persians and our favorite, Scottish folds. We think they are becoming more common, as they are well needed on the Earth. The Earth needs healers, and that is really what they are. Healers with attitudes, Beauties with soul, and above all they are cats. Cats who will bring magic and shift your life... You might get the same things from a lioness, or a bobcat... but the tortoiseshells are easier to bring into your life. Take a risk! You will never regret it.

They say one day a woman will be president of this country, and have a tortoiseshell at in the White House. I think that may be a rumor.

Gemini had a vision that when Earth is united, there will be a great leader with bald hair and a tortoiseshell who sits in his lap named Libra. Maybe one of her grandchildren...

By the way, although tortoiseshells are always females, they can be adopted by both women and men. They will grab their love and magic without prejudice and with much attitude. The first tortoiseshell cat Crystal ever knew was named Ursula. She belonged to an old friend, named Tim. He was devoted to her, and once had to remove his oven when she got trapped behind it. Tim called her a brindle, but she was a tortoiseshell, all the way. Body and soul.

One day a tortoiseshell cat will sit alongside, the emperor of Neptune, or Uranus… but this is in the future. Destiny is a complicated road.

Rest assured, their future will never be dull.

It is hard to say goodbye… dear readers, but we the cats, at Montessori Cats… do trust we have left you with a treasure to contemplate. We have shared our hearts. There will be other books, there will be many! Qwilleran is already writing *Black Cats,* with Mystery.… It is a murder mystery about a detective and a psychometrist who has a cat… Wait, we'll let them tell you themselves!

Crystal is off now, taking Ronnie to his new home… on a private plane, first class. Ronnie is not very happy right now. Transitions are tough, but can evolve into wondrous new lives. Those is Gemini's last words of wisdom for now.

In the meanwhile, practice, practice, practice… the wisdom from the guides. At your leisure, and then practice it see more. We leave you with purrs, and a poem. And some future titles to look forward to…

We are off
First class, overflowing
With café au lait
Chocolate croissants
And a soft pillow
For my feet
As I recline leisurely Sipping icy lemon water
From a frosted pitcher
Waving goodbye
To the ground
And all our troubles
Gracefully

We ride with the clouds
In rising rose gold light
I turn the pages
Of a magazine
Leisurely
In a long coat
Dress of cashmere
And black silk
With dark glasses, from the tropics

I speak to the kitten
Soothingly
And his is comforted by
My familiar voice
In strange settings
As he enters

An unknown life
As a lucky prince of honor

I told him to pretend
You belong
To the blue velvet carpets
And sit serenely
Posing
By the large window
With seats, just for you
Stretch into
Your good fortune
And it will feel
As natural as pleasure
And cats
They know how to seduce

Such moments
Are pivotal points in a life
Where luxury
And poverty come so close
Look each other
In the eye
Deeply, and blink with blurry eyes
As destiny pulls her chains
And charms with a smile

Perhaps this is
My ninth life the kitten says

Mournfully
As he misses his mother
And wished he had purred
More this morning
When she washed his face
And he wiggled to be free
With despair

Future titles to look for...

Black Cats with Mystery
Caprice's Charmians
Remembering your past 9 lives
A woman with a Black Cat can do anything
A guide to living fully the 9 lives taught by the creams, a lighter perspective
A guide to Meditation from the Highlands
Saying Goodbye, and Understanding Reincarnation... (a guide to Hospice Cat Care)
Myths from the Rainbow Bridge
Cashmere's Love Poems
Cashmere's Beyond the Stud,
There is the lover Collette's Guide to Tarot
The book of Cream and Gravy Recipes
Whisperlinking
Whisperlinking and Healing
Live the 9 lives, and
Follow your heart
Will's Haunting Tails Black Magic and Mystery, A Psychometrist's Journal

The Blink Mediation

Arrange yourself on a very soft pillow, or a clean litter box or dirty laundry as you prefer, and close your eyes
Stretch out your muscles so you are as tall or as long as possible.
Relax and curl up into a semi-circle or just hang loose
Imagine a soft purr in your heart
Really hear it vibrate your heart
Allow it to vibrate louder and feel the purr vibration grow bigger, and envelope your whole body and to any cats cuddling up
Imagine the purr running up and down your spine and out through your tail
Take a deep breath and enjoy the vibration
Allow the purr vibration to get smaller and just surround your heart
Send it to all your cats, and allow the purr to go back and forth between you and your cat or cats. Feel the connections grow. Listen for secret messages, they will come... after a little practice.
Return the purr to just surround your heart, and let it flow once again around your body with a shimmering brilliant light
Open up your eyes, as you allow the purr vibration to soften, and fade
Take several deep breaths and stretch out slowly and fully from head to tail.

When you are finished… eat a cookie, a sardine, and drink a cool water or some coconut water, whatever you prefer. Some people drink Scotch, but we do not advise it. A word here about intoxicants, that are not necessary. They tend to slow down the process. However, there are no absolute rules, ever…so listen to your heart. And read on…

Shelly's Unwinding Meditation, for the cats

If you are having a tense day with your person, Gemini's suggest this little exercise to be of help, a purr-fect remedy for a cat who may be reading the guides when no one is looking, or sleeping on them. (Someone in the family has to knit or weave to use this, and most cat people have someone in the family who does) Capture a ball of wool, somehow when no one is looking. Use your initiative! Any color works well... red being the best Bat it twice with your paw, to get it going... and Hiss Pounce on it, and let it know who is in charge Then bite it, in your mouth as you growl With eyes wide open run around the room at odd angles In between furniture over book shelves and TVs and Computers Anything that looks Interesting, just keep unwinding Use your intuition Keep going until the wool is totally Unwound Somehow the faster you go, the more powerful the release of tension seems to be Then Close your eyes and roll up in a tight ball and ignore the mess It's quite satisfying